THE STATE'S WITNESS 2

No Way Out

KYIRIS ASHLEY

URBAN AINT DEAD PRESENTS

URBAN AINT DEAD

P.O Box 960780
Riverdale GA., 30296

Cover Design: Akirecover2cover.com

Edited By: Artessa Michele-Thomas / Editing 01

URBAN AINT DEAD and coinciding logo(s) are registered properties.

Contact Author on FB: Kyiris Ashley / IG: @kyirisashley

Contact Publisher at www.urbanaintdead.com

Email: urbanaintdead@gmail.com

Print ISBN: 979-8-9888415-0-0

Ebook ISBN: 979-8-9886522-9-8

SOUNDTRACK

Scan the QR Code below to listen to the Soundtracks/Singles of some of your favorite U.A.D titles:

Don't have Spotify or Apple Music?
No Sweat!
Visit your choice streaming platform and search URBAN AINT DEAD.

Currently on lock serving a bid?
JPay, iHeartRadio, WHATEVER!
We got you covered.
Simply log into your facility's kiosk or tablet, go to music and search URBAN AINT DEAD.

URBAN AINT DEAD

Like & Follow us on social media:

FB – URBAN AINT DEAD

IG: @urbanaintdead

Tik Tok - @urbanaintdead

SUBMISSION GUIDELINES

Submit the first three chapters of your completed manuscript to urbanaintdead@gmail.com, subject line: Your book's title. The manuscript must be in a .doc file and sent as an attachment. The document should be in Times New Roman, double-spaced, and in size 12 font. Also, provide your synopsis and full contact information. If sending multiple submissions, they must each be in a separate email. Have a story but no way to submit it electronically? You can still submit to URBAN AINT DEAD. Send in the first three chapters, written or typed, of your completed manuscript to:

URBAN AINT DEAD
P.O Box 960780
Riverdale GA., 30296

DO NOT send original manuscript. Must be a duplicate.
Provide your synopsis and a cover letter containing your full contact information.

Thanks for considering URBAN AINT DEAD.

CHAPTER ONE

Tianna sat inside her small dusty room, which looked more like a jail cell than a bedroom. The room had nothing inside other than a twin bed, a sink with a small mirror hanging over it, and a small wooden table with a desk lamp. There weren't any windows inside the room, so Tianna never knew if it was day or night. There was no television, no radio, no books, no means of entertainment whatsoever. There wasn't even a dresser, so all the clothes Tianna had was inside a black trash bag in the corner of the room. With nothing else to do, Tianna was stuck looking at the same four dirty walls. The only time she could leave the room was when she had a client or when she needed to use the bathroom. Sometimes, although rarely, the owners of the brothel would let the girls visit with the other girls in the building. It was then Tianna would hear the stories of the other women and how they'd gotten there. It was those times where Tianna felt thankful because no matter how bad she thought things had been for her, there was always someone worse off than she was.

Tianna sat on the edge of the bed as she nodded in and out of consciousness. She was so high she could hardly stay awake. She knew she needed to wash herself and get ready for her next client, but the heroin she'd been given made it hard for her to function. It was the only constant outlet she had to cope with the situation she'd been put in. So, she let them drug her in order to numb her pain. Tianna attempted to stand, but every time she did, she fell right back down.

"Merrni dreqin!" Agon yelled, walking into Tianna's room.

Tianna had been in Albania for over a year now and still had trouble understanding their native tongue. She looked up at the man confused, not sure what he was trying to tell her. She focused on his mouth, as if she would be able to understand what he was saying by his facial expressions, but she was so high, Agon had three faces and she didn't know which one to listen to. She stared up at his copper-colored faces and attempted to focus on just one, as his dark brown eyes starred on at her in disgust.

"I said get the fuck up!" Agon spoke again with his heavy Albanian accent.

Tianna pulled herself to her feet and stumbled over to the sink to wash up.

"What the fuck are you doing? Your customer is waiting on you. If you didn't wash that nasty pussy before now, then you ain't got time. Now, get the fuck over here and let's go. Nixito!" Agon yelled, grabbing Tianna by the arm and pulling her out the room.

They walked down the hallway filled with dirty walls and girls so high, they were passed out in their rooms on the floor. From the moment Tianna was brought over to Albania, they'd pumped her veins full of heroin, keeping her too high to do anything except lie on her back, and they were doing the same with every other girl in the brothel. It had gotten so bad that whenever Tianna didn't have the drug, her body craved it. She would itch so badly that she would break her skin when she scratched, causing nasty sores to form all over her body. Tianna's once beautifully curved body had been replaced with a drug-induced frail frame, and her hair was always matted on the top of her head. She looked nothing like the beautiful woman she once was. Russell had stripped her of everything, including her dignity, until she had nothing left.

Agon stopped at an open doorway and pushed Tianna into the small room where her client was waiting. The fishy odor from the woman before her still lingered in the air, and Tianna turned her nose up at the putrid smell. Her client wasted no time standing to his feet, walking over to Tianna, and cupping her breasts in his hands.

"Take off your clothes," the man whispered.

Tianna obliged, removing the short pink nightgown she wore and let it fall to the floor, revealing her body to the man. Smiling, he placed one of her still perky breasts into his mouth and sucked. He placed two fingers inside her, and Tianna began to moan. She could feel herself losing her balance and almost fell over as the man fingered her faster. She had to grab onto him to avoid falling onto the floor.

"Damn, are you okay?" The man asked.

"Yessss, I'mmm finnne," Tianna slurred, moving her head slowly from right to left.

"Oh, hell no! You're not fine; you're high as hell. I'm not paying good money to fuck on no high ass bitch. You can't even hold yourself up on your own two feet. I told them not to bring me anyone that was on drugs, paid extra just to make sure of it. I'm sending your ass back!" The man yelled.

Tianna sobered up quickly at the mention of him sending her back. She knew if he did, she would be beaten by Agon for losing money. She couldn't take another beating. The last one he'd given her almost put her in the hospital. Tianna knew she had to do whatever she could to stop him from sending her back.

"No, I'm not, daddy. It was just feeling real good and I was enjoyin' it. I didn't want you to stop daddy," Tianna cooed.

He looked her over once more, making sure she was indeed telling the truth. She seemed to be fine to him, so he preceded to have his way with her, fucking Tianna for hours until he no longer had enough energy to stand. When he was done, he sat on the edge of the bed and smoked a cigarette. It took everything in him to muster up enough energy to put his clothes back on.

Tianna went straight to her room and grabbed a towel and a change of clothes. She had been too high to shower after her last two clients and could feel the stickiness between her legs. A lot of the girls in the brothel didn't care about how they smelled, but Tianna wanted to make sure she at least stayed fresh no matter how high she was. In her eyes, just because she looked like a dope fiend didn't mean she had to smell like one. That alone set her apart from the rest of the girls there and made more of the clients request her services above all others.

She stood in the small bathroom looking at herself in the mirror; her hair was a mess and hadn't been touched in months. When she'd first gotten to Albania, she was too depressed to keep her appearance up to par. After that, she'd just simply been too high. Turning on the shower, she grabbed the shampoo and a bar of soap and began washing herself. Tianna dried her hair and used a pair of scissors to cut off all the dreads that had formed in her hair, until she was left with her once signature short haircut. Once she was fully clothed, she placed gel in her hair and brushed it to the back, leaving her with a slick-back style. She even laid her baby hairs to give it more of a styled look. When she was done, she went back to her room ready for her next hit of heroin. Although she wanted to stop, she was afraid that if she did, the pain of what was happening to her would actually feel real.

———

Nikki walked into her motel room holding several Kroger bags. She knew she needed to save money, and eating out every day would make that harder. So, she went to the grocery store to stock her mini fridge with things she liked. Once she put her items away, she went into the bathroom to shower. Nikki was thankful she'd ran into one of her old johns. If it wasn't for him, she wouldn't even have a place to lay her head. He'd gotten her a room at a motel for the next two weeks and told her he would help her as much as he could.

With her eighteenth birthday still several months away, she knew she wouldn't be able to get her own apartment unless it was in someone else's name. So, for now, the best she could do was the small motel room. She knew Russell was still out there somewhere trying to find her. The constant not knowing if she would run into him one day had her anxiety through the roof. Nikki would wear fitted caps and sunglasses every time she left her room as though she was a fugitive, and in a way, she was. She knew if Russell found her, she would either be facing death or twenty-five to life in an Albanian brothel. Nikki couldn't do either, so she would watch her back and look over her shoulder until she no longer had to.

Cole, the john that had been so nice to her, let her know that he would supply anything she would need and had been doing that thus far. Too afraid to work after Shamia's death, Nikki had quit her job at the Coney Island and was relying on Cole as her main source of survival. When he was around, Nikki felt safe, as if she could trust him with her life. In a way, she already was because all Cole would have to do was give one word to Russell, and Nikki's life would be over just like that. However, Nikki knew that was a chance she would have to take. At the moment, Cole was her only lifeline and she could only hope he kept his word.

Although he was nice and taking care of her, Nikki didn't really like having sex with Cole. He was always too overemotional during the act, wanting to hear Nikki tell him she loved him and telling him she belonged to him. Nikki had never been a good actress but deserved an Academy Award for the role she was playing with Cole. Knowing if she didn't play her role, she would lose everything, and she couldn't have that. If nothing else, Nikki had to stay with him until her eighteenth birthday when she could get a place of her own.

———

"Oh, my God, my baby! Please, I need to go to the hospital!" Nakia yelled, rolling onto her back and cradling her stomach with both hands.

Nakia sat up and leaned her back against the tub. The pain that she was feeling was almost unbearable and she knew something had to be wrong. Nakia had given birth to two other children and had never felt anything remotely close to this pain before. When her water broke with Rashaud and Lexi, it was clear fluid running from between her legs. However, this time, when Nakia placed her hand between her thighs, her palms were stained with deep crimson.

"Bitch, you not even gonna make it out this house alive, let alone to no fuckin' hospital!" Niko yelled before hitting Nakia in the face with the butt of his gun.

Nakia fell over onto her side and onto the glass for the shattered lamp. She screamed loudly, both out of fear and pain. Nakia could taste the blood in her mouth and knew he'd busted her lip. She looked at him with tear-stained eyes, pleading with him to let her go. Her baby needed a hospital and fast. Nakia knew she was losing a lot of blood, and if she didn't get help quickly, she and her child both could die. Nakia watched as Niko squatted down in front of her and grabbed her cheeks tightly, squeezing them together, just like a mother would do her disobedient child.

"I'm gonna enjoy killin' you. If it's one thing I hate, it's a bitch that can't mind her own business. I bet you think twice about openin' yo mouth next time. Then, again, you can't talk if you dead," Niko laughed sinisterly.

Nakia knew this was the end for her; it was nothing more she could do but accept her fate. Taking a deep breath, she silently prayed for God to watch over her children and shield their hearts from the pain of losing their mother. Growing up in foster care, she knew the dark side parentless children faced and didn't want that for her children. She knew Jalyn would take them in and care for them as his own; however, she wished things could be different. If she could rewind time, she would go back to the day she called the police and would have never made the call. As if her prayer had been answered, she was shown a way out. There right beside her was a piece of glass from the broken lamp. Thinking quick on her feet, Nakia grabbed the glass and shoved it directly into the left side of Niko's neck, twisted it, and pulled it out. Blood splattered all over Nakia's face and bathroom wall before Niko even knew what was happening.

Dropping his gun on the floor, Niko placed his hand up to his neck and blood poured down his shoulder and chest. He attempted to speak, but no words came out as he choked on his own blood. Nakia quickly scooted away from Niko, and he fanatically tried to pull a towel from the towel rack in an attempt to stop the bleeding. Nakia watched as Niko's knees became weak and he had to stand against the wall in order not to fall to the ground.

Nakia looked in his eyes and saw them pleading for her to help him. However, Nakia didn't move, just looked on at Niko's lips as they began to turn purple. No longer being able to stand, Niko slowly slid down the wall, leaving a trail of blood behind him. They both knew he was dying, and for Nakia, that was her only way out. Once Niko passed out, Nakia knew she had to make a run for it, at least making it down to her phone to call for help.

Placing one hand on the toilet and the other on the bathtub, Nakia forced herself to stand to her feet. She winced from the pain with each step she took; however, Nakia kept walking. Blood ran down her legs and onto the floor as she made her way through the hallway towards the stairs. She'd just made it to the top of the steps when the front door opened and Raphael walked in.

"Raphael, I need help!" Nakia yelled frantically as she looked down at him.

Without a word, Raphael quickly ran to her, confused about what was happening. It wasn't until he got to the top of the stairs that he saw that Nakia was cover in blood. His heart began beating rapidly as he looked at her, trying to figure out where the blood was coming from.

"Baby, what happened?" Raphael asked.

"I need to go to the hospital. There's a man in our bathroom, and I think he's dead. I killed him, Raphael, or at least I think I did. It's something wrong with the baby, get me to the hospital."

Tears began to pour down Nakia's face, as Raphael lifted her into his arms. Raphael had no idea what went on, and all he could think about was getting Nakia to the hospital as quickly as possible. He rushed to the car without giving a second thought to Nakia saying it was a dead body in their bathroom. At that moment, his only concern was the health and safety of his future wife and unborn child.

CHAPTER TWO

"Tell me this pussy is mine," Cole moaned as he pumped in and out of Nikki. Instead of answering, Nikki continued to move her hips in small circles. She knew Cole loved when she did that, and it always brought him to his climax faster. The faster he came, the faster he would be out of Nikki, and that's all she wanted. She knew without Cole, she wouldn't have much of anything; however, she didn't want him either. Nikki had already told herself once she turned eighteen, she wasn't going to fuck with Cole anymore. However, she felt for the time being, she didn't have a choice.

"Shit, baby, tell me you love me. This pussy so good to me. I need you to love me," he continued.

Nikki rolled her eyes and didn't say a word. *I wish he would stop that shit, ain't nobody trying to be in love with his ass. This is only supposed to be sex for support, not lovemaking and togetherness,* Nikki thought to herself. Before she knew it, Cole had busted his nut and was now breathing heavily as he laid on top of her.

"Damn baby, that shit be so good to me. You can't give this shit to nobody else but me. I'ma be all you ever gon' need boo, I promise," Cole spoke.

"I gotta get in the shower," Nikki replied.

"Yeah, I'ma join you. I'm not ready to let you go just yet," Cole stated, getting up from the bed and walking into the bathroom.

Nikki walked in slowly after him and turned on the water. She thought he would leave when they were done; however, Cole clearly had plans to stick around. She wanted to tell him to leave but was scared he might get mad and stop helping her. Nikki wouldn't know what to do if Cole really cut her off so, instead of finding out, she smiled, and they both stepped into the running water.

"You need to start lookin' for an apartment or somethin'. I'm sick of this little ass room. It's been too long; plus, we can't do shit in this muthafucka. You can go from the bed to the bathroom in five steps," Cole stated.

Nikki's eyes widened at the statement and a huge smile spread across her face. Nikki having her own apartment was exactly what she needed. She would feel much more comfortable in a bigger space that she could call her own. *Maybe fuckin' with Cole ain't that bad. Hell, if this nigga gonna get me a place and help pay my bills, I'll fuck him good every night,* Nikki thought as she lathered her body with soap. Even though she wasn't attracted to Cole sexually, Nikki knew how to play her role. For a place to call her own, that's exactly what Nikki would do.

Once out the shower, Nikki dressed in her pajamas and laid out on the bed. She searched her phone for different rental listings until she came across a few she liked. She showed Cole, and he told her they could set up appointments the following day to tour the apartments. Nikki fell asleep that night with a smile on her face. She was so happy, she didn't even protest when Cole wrapped his arms around her and pulled her closer, cuddling her close well into the night.

That next morning, they went to see three apartments and a house. Nikki quickly settled on the three-bedroom house, which was newly renovated and had new appliances throughout. Nikki loved the open layout of the home and couldn't wait to begin the decorating process. With the house being rented out by a private owner, Cole was able to pay extra in order for them to get the keys the same day. Nikki was happy as she walked through Wal-Mart with Cole, picking up everything she would need to be comfortable for the next few days until her furniture was delivered.

"I'ma call DTE tomorrow and have the lights and gas put into my name. I'll call and get the Wi-Fi turned on as well. You know I'ma need some Netflix and shit in my life," Cole stated.

"Okay, cool, thanks. I really appreciate everything you're doing for me, Cole. I don't know where I would be right now if I didn't see you at the restaurant that night," Nikki assured genuinely.

"You my girl, I'ma always make sure you have whatever you need. I'm never gonna let you go without. I got you for life baby."

Nikki chuckled as she smiled weakly. Not one time did she tell this man she was his girl. She wanted to let him know they were not in a relationship, but there was no way she could. This man had just blew several bags on her getting her a place to stay. With that, Nikki felt obligated to give him exactly what her wanted. So, if her being his girl was what he wanted, Nikki had no choice but to oblige.

———

"What do you mean the baby might not make it? Where is Nakia?" Jalyn asked frantically as he paced back and forth.

Raphael didn't know what to say. He had no clue what happened; all he knew was he wasn't there to protect her or his child. He didn't even have the words to explain that to Jalyn, so he had no idea what he would tell the children. Raphael's emotions ran rapid as the many unanswered questions ran through his mind. He felt so helpless as he sat in the waiting room of Beaumont Hospital.

"They both in surgery, her and the baby. I'm not sure what happened. She went to drop the kids off to Simone, and I went to chill with my pops. When I got back, she was on the stairs with blood all over her. I brought her straight here," Raphael replied, shaking his head in confusion.

He dropped his head low and ran his hands over his Creaser. He could only pray that his family would make it out safely and healthy. He couldn't lose Nakia, and the mere thought of that happening had Raphael going insane. He'd spent his entire life looking for his soul mate, and now that he'd found her, he couldn't let her slip through his fingers. Worry filled his heart, as a single tear ran down his cheek. *Fuck would I do without her?* he thought.

"Was she alert when you found her? Did she say anything to you before they took her back to surgery? I'ma need you to tell me more," Jalyn asked.

"Yes, she was awake."

"Then, what the fuck did she say happened?" Jalyn asked again, becoming upset at the fact he wasn't getting the answers he was requesting.

Raphael thought for a moment as he replayed the events back in his head moment by moment. He'd been so caught up in getting Nakia to the hospital that what actually had taken place went over his head. Raphael was just about to speak when a doctor walked up to the two of them.

"Are you family of Nakia Pitchford?"

"Yes, I'm her fiancé and he is her brother," Raphael introduced as he stood to his feet.

"My name is Dr. Sutton and I oversaw Nakia's surgery. Everything went smoothly and she's resting right now. You two should be able to see her in a few moments," she said with a smile.

"And the baby?" Raphael asked.

"I'm not sure. The children's cardiologist is over the newborn's surgery. As soon as I have some information about him, I'll let you know. If you two will follow me, I'll take you to Nakia. She is still very weak and might not wake up for a few hours; however, the two of you are more than welcome to sit in with her."

Raphael's heart broke when he walked into the hospital room and saw Nakia. Her beautiful face was swollen and had black and purple bruises all over it. He hadn't noticed them before, but looking at her face now angered him. He quickly walked over to her, grabbing her hand and placing a soft kiss on her forehead.

"I'm here baby," Raphael whispered.

"I'll leave you two alone with her," Dr. Sutton informed.

Jalyn pulled a chair over to Nakia's bed and sat on the opposite side. He couldn't believe he was sitting in his sister's hospital room, waiting for her to wake up. He wanted to scream, cry, and blow shit up all at once. Nakia was the sweetest soul he knew, and he couldn't figure out who would want to do something so horrible to her. Anger shot through his body as he looked up at Raphael.

"Who you got lookin' for you?"

"What?" Raphael asked, confused.

"I said, who the fuck you got lookin' for you? My sista don't have no fuckin' enemies. So, I'ma ask you again, who the fuck is lookin' for you?" Jalyn said through clenched teeth.

Raphael looked up at Jalyn, livid at the assumption he had anything to do with Nakia being hurt. He would give his life twice over for Nakia, so how the hell could Jalyn even think he could be the cause of her pain? He knew that Jalyn was angry and scared, hell, so was he. However, blaming him for what happened would not help the situation at all.

"Listen Jay, I know you are looking for someone to blame, but I'm not the one. We both know if I was there, this wouldn't have happened at all. And when I find out who did this, it's up," Raphael replied.

"Nigga, my sista never had these types of problems. The only thing different in her life is you! I should be putting yo ass out right now. Matter fact, nigga, get out!" Jalyn yelled, standing to his feet.

He balled his fist, ready to swing on Raphael if he protested. His sister had clearly been severely beaten, and although he couldn't prove it, he knew Raphael had something to do with it.

"I'm not going anywhere! I'm not leaving until my wife and child are both safe. Now, I need you to lower your voice; this is a hospital Jay, have some respect."

Raphael knew Jalyn was scared, however, so was he. So, there was no way he was just gonna sit there and tolerate disrespect.

"She ain't yo fuckin' wife yet, and she won't be if I have something to do with it. She will always be my sista though, so I'm gonna always protect her. You, on the other hand, will have her laying in fuckin' hospital beds like she is now!" Jalyn yelled.

Raphael had enough of Jalyn and his shit-talking. He stood to his feet and walked over to Jalyn. They stared each other down, and it took everything in Raphael not to knock some act right into Jalyn.

"Please y'all, stop," a voice whispered weakly.

Jalyn and Raphael both stopped in their tracks and looked over at Nakia. They ran over to the bed and sat beside her, happy that she was now awake.

"Babe, I'm so happy that you're awake," Raphael whispered as he placed gentle kisses on the back of Nakia's hand.

"Sis, what happened? Who beat you up? Tell me and I'ma handle it for you," Jalyn asked.

"I need water, my throat is too dry and it hurts to talk," she answered.

Jalyn rushed to the table in the corner of the room and poured Nakia a cup of water. He placed a straw in the cup, then placed the straw to her lips. Nakia sucked as though she'd been in a desert for days without water, feeling relief as the cool liquid lubricated her throat.

"Where is the baby?" she asked, looking directly at Raphael.

"He's still in surgery; the doctor will let us know as soon as he's out.

Nakia smiled at the mention of the baby being a boy. She had a dream for Lexi to be her only daughter, and as of now, that dream was still very much a reality.

"Sis, what the hell happened to you? You got me over here trippin'," Jalyn asked.

"I don't know. One minute I was in the tub waiting on Raphael to get home, so we could have dinner. Next thing I know, it was a man in the house pistol whippin' me. I'd never seen the man in my life and had no clue who he was."

"A man did this to you? Where the fuck is he now? Raphael, did you see him?" Jalyn asked.

"He's dead, I killed him," Nakia cried, as the realization of what she'd done set in.

Raphael's eyes widened as things began to come back to him. His main focus had been to get Nakia to the hospital. It was only then that he remembered Nakia telling him someone was in their bathroom dead. With everything going on, he'd completely forgotten about that.

"We need to call the police. I killed a man," Nakia continued.

"Sis, just calm down. You just got out of surgery; I don't want you getting yourself all worked up. What makes you think you killed him?" Jalyn asked, convinced his sister was mistaken.

"I stabbed him in the neck. It was so much blood, there's no way he's still alive," Nakia wept as she placed her hands over her face in an effort to cover her tears.

"Hell nah, sis, we ain't calling no police. You know I don't fuck with them. That man probably not even dead," Jalyn stated, holding his hands up in disagreement.

"What, are you crazy? We have to call them. It's a fucking dead man in my bathroom. I killed him, Jay. We have to call the police because it's the right thing to do. Raphael, please call them."

Raphael pulled his phone from his pocket and nodded his head okay. He turned to walk out the room, and Jalyn walked in front of him, stopping him in his tracks.

"Fuck you doing man? We can't call the fuckin' boyz. You out yo fuckin' mind dawg," Jalyn stated.

"Relax Jay, I got this," Raphael whispered before walking out the room.

Raphael was not the type of man to call no damn police. His father had people who could handle anything, and that's exactly who Raphael called. When Fatbar answered on the second ring, Raphael began telling him everything that happened.

"What's the address? I'll have Niko go handle it right now. I'm sure he's finished with his job by now," Fatbar stated.

After jotting down the address, he got the location of the hospital and told Raphael that he and Harlin would be there shortly. Raphael ended the call and walked back into Nakia's room. Thoughts of what the man was doing in his home ran through his head. *Was this just a random robbery gone wrong?* With Raphael's line of work, he knew it could be a number of reasons as to why the man was really there. Whatever the reason, Raphael would damn sure find out. He wouldn't rest until whoever had done this to Nakia and their child felt the same pain they did.

CHAPTER THREE

Tianna walked out of the room after leaving her tenth client of the day. Her vagina ached from being pounded in several different ways. She knew she needed to get the hell out of Albania, however, she didn't know how. Even if she made it past all the security at the brothel, how would she get back to America? She had no money, no passport and no way to get either. Tianna knew she had to figure out something, but until then, she had no choice but to stay at the brothel.

After showering, Tianna walked back into her room to find her dinner sitting on the small table. Seeing how they were only given one meal at the end of their shift, Tianna was starving. She grabbed the plate and began to eat, letting the food give her body much needed nourishment. Once she was done eating, she sat her plate outside her door and got in bed. She went to sleep with thoughts of an escape deep in her mind.

Tianna was awakened in the middle of the night by Tiny. Tiny was one of the few girls in the brothel who Tianna actually got along with. Tianna would even go far enough to say they were friends. Tiny was coco brown with jet black hair and a body to die for. She stood four-eleven, the reason she received the nickname "Tiny".

"Tianna, please get up; we need your help! Hurry please, before it's too late!" Tiny yelled frantically.

Tianna was startled by the urgency in which she was woken up. It took her several seconds to process what was even going on. When she heard Tiny tell her again that she needed her help, Tianna jumped out of bed and followed Tiny out the room. They ran down the stairs to the lower level of the building until they got to Dahlia's room. Dahlia was a white girl that had been sold there about a month ago. Although Dahlia didn't really talk to anyone, everyone knew she was having a really hard time coming to terms with being at the brothel. The story was she was sold by a man she thought was her boyfriend, and the betrayal sent her into a depression.

When they walked inside the room, Tianna saw Dahlia lying on the floor of the room. Her skin was purple and her eyes seemed to be bulging out of her head. Two other girls sat on the floor beside her, one of them administering CPR. Tianna looked at the rope that hung from a steel bar in the ceiling and knew she'd hung herself. Lowering her head and closing her eyes, Tianna paid her respects to the young girl's life.

"She's already gone y'all, it's nothing we gonna be able to do," Tianna whispered.

"Nooo, please! We have to save her," Tiny cried.

"She's right; it's nothing we can do. It's too late," one of the other girls said, as she stood from the floor.

Tiny cried as she shook her head in disbelief. She hated that Dahlia's life had been cute short due to her circumstances. She wished she'd gotten there sooner and was able to talk Dahlia out of doing something so horrible. However, the reality was she hadn't, and the results of that were tragic. Tiny, not being able to take the sight of Dahlia's dead body any longer, stormed out the room. Tianna followed behind her as she called out her name.

"Tiny, wait up, girl," Tianna whispered, not wanting to wake up the house guards.

Tiny stopped, standing there crying as she waited on Tianna. "She didn't deserve that shit. Why wouldn't they just let her go home? They have dozens of girls in here, that one leaving wouldn't have made a difference. This shit is fucked up," Tiny stated.

"Let's go back to my room, we don't need to be caught out here in the hallway like this."

The two walked back to Tianna's room, and she closed the door behind them.

"I wanna leave too, but how can we? Where would we go? If we escaped from here, there is no way we could stay in Albania after that. They have eyes everywhere," Tianna stated.

"My friend can get us out," Tiny informed.

Tianna looked over at Tiny, perplexed. *What the fuck did she just say? If she has a way for us to leave, then why the fuck are we still here?* Tianna thought.

"Bitch, who you know that can get us out of here?" Tianna asked.

"Darden, he's in love with me. He's been telling me for months that he could get us to the U.S., so we could live a happy life," Tiny informed.

"Darden? The dude that delivers the food to us?" Tianna asked.

"Yeah, that's him. We want to be together and we know we can't do it here. He came up with a plan to get us into the U.S. and he's just waiting on me to tell him I'm ready."

"Then, what are you waiting on?" Tianna inquired.

"I've been scared. Scared of what would happen to me if we got caught. But after tonight, I don't give a fuck any more. I'm ready to go, and if you want, you can come with us," Tiny replied.

"What's the plan?"

Tiny ran down the plan to Tianna, as she listened to every detail. Tianna smiled for the first time, as a glimmer of hope sparkled in her mind. The plan sounded fool-proof, and she knew it would work. However, would Darden let Tianna tag along with him and Tiny? If he did, could Tianna even trust him? There was a lot of things running through Tianna's mind at that moment, and she needed to get the answers to her questions.

"Do you think Darden will meet with me? I need for him to tell me it's okay for me to go with y'all. I don't need no damn surprises," Tianna asked.

Tiny nodded her head, telling Tianna she would have Darden come and speak with her the following evening. Tianna agreed, happy that she could possibly be going back home. She only prayed that Darden would indeed let her leave with them. The two women said goodnight to each other before Tiny walked out the room.

———

Russell laid in bed thinking about his victory. In his eyes, he'd cheated the law, and they now had nothing on him. He couldn't wait until the day the judge said "case dismissed". He needed to get back to the money, but he couldn't do that if he was still under the feds' watchful eye. Travis wasn't being any help either. Russell was now questioning if he could even trust him anymore, which saddened him because Travis was his brother. He'd been on some real shady shit the past few days, and Russell was praying he wasn't talking to the police. He tried to shrug it off as just him being paranoid, but something inside him was telling him his thoughts were true. He was always taught to listen to his first mind, and his first mind was telling him his brother was a snitch.

Getting out of bed, Russell made his way to the kitchen to get something to eat. He was halfway through the living room when he heard Travis whispering to someone. When he didn't hear another voice, he assumed Travis was on the phone. Russell listened to as much of the conversation as he could, only to find out his brother was trying to spit game to some bitch he met around the way. Russell was relived and continued to walk into the kitchen.

"Yo baby, let me hit you back later. I'm bout to holla at my bro real quick. I'll call you when I'm bout to be on my way," Travis stated.

"What you up to bro? What lil bitch you bout to go get in tonight?" Russell joked

"This lil high yellow freak I met in the hood last week. She fine as hell bro, thick ass lil bitch. I know I'ma feel what that gushy like tonight, and I can't wait."

"You tryin' to put her down with the team?" Russell asked.

"Hell nah, this a lil bitch that I'm tryin' ta kick it wit'. Everybody I meet is not for your business Russell'; I got a life too," Travis spoke.

Russell didn't say a word, just looked at him and nodded his head. He made himself a sandwich, grabbed a bottle of water and made his way back to his room. He wasn't gonna even play into Travis' bullshit attitude. Sitting back on his bed, he began going through Instagram, looking for potential females so he could reconstruct his roster. Once he did so, he would get another Airbnb and cut ties with Travis' shady ass. The only girl he had left on his team was Hannah, and although she was a down ass bitch, it was only so much she could do. The amount of money she was bringing in on the daily was barely making the bills. After paying Fatbar for his services, Russell didn't have any savings left, so he knew he needed to make a power move quickly.

After sending a few DMs out, he texted Hannah to come to his room. He needed to get his mind off of whatever Travis might be doing, and Hannah was the perfect way. He knew once she entered his room, she would suck all his troubles away. Russell hated the very thought of having to take out his brother. However, he knew that if his brother snitched, then that was exactly what he would have to do.

———

"I can't get in touch with Niko. I've been trying to call him the entire way here. I ended up calling Manny to have him handle it. Niko must still be on that job I sent him on," Fatbar whispered.

Manny was Niko's younger brother but was just as good at the game as Niko was, so Fatbar knew everything would be straight. Anytime Fatbar sent any one of his nephews on a job, he knew they would execute it perfectly, so he had nothing to worry about on that end. His main concern was the safety of Nakia and his grandchild.

Raphael nodded his head, as he sat in a chair staring at the wall. He and Nakia had just been informed their son was out of surgery but would still be in the NICU for at least several more weeks. Although he was happy the surgery went well, he was still nervous about the care his baby still had to receive. He wanted nothing more than to take his baby boy home, and now they were telling him that wasn't possible.

"I brought coffee for everyone," Harlin announced as she walked inside the waiting room.

"I'm good ma, thanks though," Raphael stated, hold his hand up and refusing the coffee.

Harlin gave a half smile as she nodded her head okay. She couldn't image what her son was feeling at the moment and wished she could ease his pain. She knew the type of man her son was, so she knew he was blaming himself for what happened to Nakia and their son and wished she had the solution to the entire problem. She was just getting ready to say something to lighten the mood when she noticed the look on Fatbar's face. She didn't know who was on the other end of that phone call, but she knew it was bad news. Sitting the coffee down on the table, she walked over to Fatbar but was halted in her tracks by a woman's loud mouth.

"Where is Nakia and the baby? I need to see my best friend right now!" Simone yelled as she walked into the waiting room.

"She's in her room resting right now, and the baby is out of surgery," Jalyn informed, standing from his seat and walking over to Simone. "Where are the kids?" he continued.

"They're at my house. I called my sister to come watch them as soon as you called me. How is she? I need to see her. At least lay my eyes on her and know that she's okay.

Jalyn nodded his head and escorted Simone to Nakia's room. Simone broke down as soon as she walked in and saw Nakia's battered face. She couldn't believe someone had done such a horrible thing to her friend, and Simone's heart ached for her. Slowly, Simone walked over to her bedside and took Nakia's hand into hers.

"I'm so sorry this happened to you," Simone whispered, with tears rolling down her cheeks.

"Bitch, why you cryin' like you the one got yo ass beat?" Nakia chucked, trying to lighten the mood.

Simone laughed and wiped her tears, as they continued to fall from her eyes. She forced a smile upon her face as she pulled up a chair and sat next to Nakia.

"I just need you to be okay, friend," Simone answered.

"I'm fine, I just want my baby to be okay. They won't let me see him until tomorrow and that shit got me going crazy. I'll be okay once I see him. What about Rashaud and Lexi, you didn't tell them I was in the hospital, did you?"

"Hell nah, you know I wouldn't do no shit like that. They at the house with my sister."

"Good, I don't want them to know what happened. Can they stay with you for a few more days? At least until my bruises get light enough for me to cover with make-up," Nakia said.

"Yeah, I got you. Don't even worry 'bout it, sis."

Nakia smiled and thanked her friend. She was thankful for the support system she had; however, she was now scared for them. Russell had indeed sent someone to kill her, and although she'd escaped that time, she knew it was only a matter of time before he came back. She would be damned if someone she loved got hurt because of her. She knew she would have to tell Raphael everything that happened. She'd just had to kill a man that came into their home to kill her. What if her other children would have been home at the time and had gotten hurt? Nakia would have never been able to forgive herself. Her son was already fighting for his life, and it was killing Nakia knowing it was all her fault.

———

Manny pulled up to the address Fatbar had given him and parked down the street. He didn't want anyone seeing him entering the home, just in case someone heard any commotion and had already alerted the authorities. Manny jogged around back and picked the lock to the door before entering the house. Walking through the family room, he noticed pictures of his cousin Raphael with his girl and children. Manny smiled at how happy the family looked. Checking every room downstairs in search of the body his uncle sent him to clean up, he had come up empty handed. Manny looked around confused as nothing looked out of place. It wasn't until he began walking up the stairs that he seen the trail of blood.

"Damn, that's a lot of blood, fuck went on in here?" Manny spoke out loud to himself, as he walked through the halls looking at the blood trail on the floor and walls.

Manny continued to follow the blood all the way to the master bedroom, where there looked to have been a struggle. He saw the broken-down door and the turned over furniture. *Man, whoever did this shit is lucky they already dead and I didn't get to them first.* Manny was furious just looking at the amount of damage that was done and could only image how scared Nakia had to be, especially knowing she was home alone when it happened. It was family over everything to Manny, and the fact Nakia was marrying his cousin made her just that.

Shaking his head, he walked into the master bathroom, still looking for the body he'd yet to find. Walking into the bathroom, he immediately was taken aback by the amount of blood on the floor, walls and toilet. There was broken glass everywhere, which crunched under his shoes as he walked in. There was so much blood that it looked like a slaughter house, and Manny knew he would have to go to great lengths to clean up this mess. It wasn't until he'd walked all the way into the bathroom that he saw the unthinkable. There, sitting on the floor with his back pressed against the wall, was the lifeless body of his only brother Niko.

"What the fuck? Niko, get up bro!" Manny yelled out, rushing over to Niko and kneeling down beside him.

"Bro, please nooooo! This shit can't be real. Niko, please get up!" Manny cried.

Realizing there was no life left in his brother, Manny stood up, punching the wall with so much force that his fist went through it. Tears flowed from his eyes freely as he screamed out in agony. He stared down at the lifeless body of his only brother in disbelief, as both pain and anger consumed his entire being.

"What the fuck is this? Fatbar sent me here knowing Niko was in here dead? Raphael and his bitch killed my brother? What the fuck is going on?" Manny threw punch after punch into the air as anger and rage took. He didn't understand what had led to this, but if it was a war they wanted, it was a war they would get. Here, Manny was thinking it was family over everything, when really the family was trying to kill them off one by one. Had Fatbar put the play down to have his brother murdered? Was this a set up to have him bodied also? He didn't know what to think, but he was damn sure going to find out. Pulling his phone from his pocket, Manny frantically placed a call to Fatbar, ready to find out the truth about what was going on.

———

"Are you okay, Fatbar?" Harlin asked, walking up to her husband.

"I'll be fine, I'm just worried about my grandson," Fatbar boasted.

"Yea, I am too, but God got him, so I believe he will pull though. He has your blood, so he's strong already," Harlin comforted.

She could tell her husband was taking this just as hard as they all were. She only prayed that everything would work out for the good. Her family had been through so much throughout the years and gotten through it all. However, each trial always seemed to be greater than the next. She wanted this time to be no different. Wanting everything to work out without any further heartache, Fatbar's phone rung. He stood up and walked off before taking the call.

"Hello," Fatbar answered once he knew he was out of ear range of everyone else in the waiting room.

"Yo, what the fuck is going on? If this is Raphael house, the why the fuck is Niko dead in the bathroom?" Manny yelled into the phone.

Fatbar's heart dropped in his chest as he listened to the words Manny spoke. As careful as Fatbar tried to be, he had just done the most careless thing possibly by putting his own family at risk. *Nakia is the fucking witness that Niko went to kill? Niko is dead?* Fatbar became hot, and he undid the top two buttons of his button-up shirt in an effort to cool off.

"Uncle Fatbar, did you hear what I said? Niko is fucking dead! You sent me here knowing that shit? Raphael killed my brother!" Manny yelled frantically. Anger and hurt rang throughout his tone.

"No!" Fatbar shot back. "I had no idea Niko would be the one in that house!" Fatbar began sweating profusely and his breaths became shorter. He placed his hand on his chest and massaged it in an effort to relieve the tightness. He felt as though he was going to throw up and leaned against the wall trying to hold himself up.

"Then, how the fuck did he get here? Where the fuck is Raphael? I need to talk to him now!" Manny informed as he looked down at his brother's body. The fact Niko was dead infuriated him to his core. All he could think about was not allowing this to go unpunished.

Fatbar opened his mouth to answer him, but no word came out. He felt as if the weight of five men were pushing down on his chest, and before he knew it, he fell to his knees. *Oh, my God, I think I'm having a heart attack.* Fatbar thought, as he fell face down on the floor.

"Fatbar!" Harlin yelled as she ran to her husband's side, getting the attention of everyone in the waiting room.

"We need help! Somebody help us!" Raphael called out as he rushed to his father's aid.

CHAPTER FOUR

R ussell got out the shower and wiped the steam from the bathroom mirror. He was feeling good about today, as he decided this would be the kickoff of the plan he'd put in motion. He knew the mistakes he'd made the first time around, so he knew what not to do this time. Since Hannah had turned eighteen, he decided he would no longer put any more underage girls on his roster. That was what fucked him up and got him caught up. He knew there were plenty of girls he could get to work for him; all he needed to do was get in their head. So, once he dropped Hannah off at the room he'd rented for her, he would come back home and begin networking. His goal was to have at least three more girls by the end of the week, so he had some work to do.

"Come on, let's be out," Russell stated, letting Hannah know it was time to go.

The two of them made their way to Russell's SUV and headed out to the hotel. A lot had changed since the law had gotten involved in Russell's business so, now, he had to make sure he kept his hands clean. That was why instead of bringing the girls back to his Airbnb, he'd rented one motel room for Hannah to work out of. Russell never did anything more than drop Hannah off and pick her up. He never even so much as went into the motel room with her. Once he did get more girls, he would rent a smaller Airbnb for them to work out of. There would be no more work being done where they laid their heads. There would be no more of him being seen with the girls while they worked. Russell would be completely behind the scenes, the way he should have been in the first place.

Russell had even ditched his personal IG and had begun working under Hannah's account. His name would no longer be caught up in anything else, just in case the police did start looking back at him. To Russell, his plan was fool- proof and the only way he could get back to the money. Once he dropped off Hannah, he immediately went back home and began working. He went to his room and began sending out DMs. Within an hour, one of the girls hit him back, letting him know she was interested in what he was offering. Seeing she was already in Detroit, Russell set up a time to meet with her later that day.

If everything worked out with her, Russell would be able to start her as soon as tomorrow. He wanted to make a good impression on her, so he would take her out to dinner in an effort to get to know her better. Give it more of an interview feel, as though it was a high-class job. He wanted her to feel comfortable enough to have no reservations about joining his team.

Excited about the new money he was about to receive, he got up and went to the barber shop for a fresh cut. Russell knew when you looked good, you did good, and he was all about that shit. Things were finally looking up for him, and he could smell the money being printed. While stopped a red light just a few miles away from the barber shop, he noticed something that put a sour taste in his mouth. There pulling into the police station was none other than Travis.

"I muthafuckin' knew it! That nigga is fucking snitching!" Russell yelled, pissed to know he was right about his brother.

It took everything in Russell not to pull into the parking lot after Travis. His blood boiled as he thought about his only brother going against him. That muthafucka was over his fucking house damn near everyday like he lived there, eating up his food and using his lights, gas and water, when all the while he talking to the damn police. Russell

26

had a major problem with that, and brother or no brother, he was gonna handle that shit.

Russell spent the rest of the afternoon getting himself together for his next potential employee. After his hair cut, he went home to get showered and changed. Russell dressed in a pair of black slacks with a white collared shirt. Leaving the top three buttons undone, Russell placed his gold Cuban link chain around his neck. Once he sprayed himself with Versace Dylan Blue, he was ready. Russell looked at himself one more in the mirror before heading out the door.

Thirty minutes later, Russell was walking into the doors of Prime + Proper and waited to be seated. He came early on purpose because he knew he would need a drink to calm down from the newly found information he'd stumbled upon. Even though the thought of what Travis had told the police troubled Russell, he had to push that shit to the back of his mind, at least for the time being. He needed to give his full attention to the project at hand, and that's exactly what he was going to do.

Russell watched as a thick ass yellow bone walked into the restaurant smiling and immediately knew she was there to see him. Deja's Instagram photos didn't do her any justice because she looked even better in person. Russell stood from the table and greeted Deja with a smile, as she walked over to him.

"Hello, Russell, right?" Deja asked.

"Yes, I'm Russell. I'm glad you were able to meet me here this evening. How are you doing, Deja?"

"I'm good, thanks for asking. How bout yourself?"

Russell took his seat before he answered, letting her know that everything was good. He couldn't help but to admire her beauty, as she sat in front of him. She was dressed in a black pants suit with no shirt on underneath her blazer, giving Russell a front row seat to the D-cup breasts she had sitting pretty. Her jet-black lace front was parted down the middle and hung down her back, damn near touching the top of her plump behind.

Russell was very impressed by her appearance because he wasn't use to females that dressed the way she did. Normally, they would be in tight jeans and shirts or little sexy dresses that showed more skin than it covered. However, Deja was sitting in front of him like she was there for an actual interview with a real company.

The two of them ordered drinks and appetizers while they spoke about Deja joining Russell's team. She was all for it; however, she was very up front with the things she wanted. She let Russell know she did not come to play. She would set her own prices for the services she rendered and would only split it with Russell 60/40, with Russell getting the 40. She was to be the only one that set up her dates because she was only to be put with the big-time hustlers and business-men, letting Russell know up front she wasn't cheap. She would never fuck without a condom and would never swallow any semen. However, she would also come with two other ladies that were getting the same money she was getting. What they needed from Russell was protec-tion, so that's what he would be paid to do.

Normally, there would be no way Russell would go for a bitch telling him what she would or wouldn't do. However, he could tell Deja was different, so the money she would bring in would be different, and she was coming with a team on top of that. Russell took a beat to look at the bigger picture. Deja alone could expand his business and brand. The way she looked alone would bring in bigger clients than any of the girls he ever had all put together. With that, Russell agreed to Deja's terms.

"Cool, I can call my girls and we can all have some drinks," Deja replied, pulling her phone from her clutch and shooting a quick text.

About fifteen minutes later, Russell noticed two women walking towards the table. One was beautiful and dark skinned with a full head of shoulder length tight curls. She wore a black knee-length pencil skirt with a white, sheer low-cut blouse that showed off the black lace bra she wore underneath. The other was caramel complected with long blonde hair. She sported a pair of jeans with a white mini tee, cover by a hot pink blazer and matching pink heels. Russell couldn't help but stare, as the women commanded the attention of the entire restaurant.

"Russell, these are my girls. Girls, this is Russell," Deja introduced.

"Hi, I'm Remy, it's nice to meet you," pink blazer introduced.

"It's nice to meet you as well," Russell replied, extending his hand to Remy. "And who might you be?" He asked, turning his attention to little miss see-through blouse.

"My name is Sophie," she replied.

The four of them got to know each other better over hours of appetizers and drinks. Once it was all said and done, they'd made an agreement to begin working with each other the following day.

———

Raphael felt as though he would lose his mind as he shuffled between hospital rooms. He just didn't understand how a weekend that could have been so perfect had turned into a nightmare within minutes. Although the heart attack Fatbar suffered was not fatal, it was enough to keep him in the hospital for several days. As if Nakia and the baby weren't enough, now he had his father to worry about as well. Raphael needed for things to get back to normal fast because he couldn't take another thing going wrong.

"How you holding up mama? Do you need anything... water... coffee?" Raphael asked as he walked into the room.

"All I need is for your father to be okay, that's it."

"And he will be, the doctors said he should make a full recovery," Raphael answered.

"You know, sometimes, I think this family has some kind of curse put upon us or something. First, it was Nakia and the baby, now this. Fatbar's mother told me this would happen. The day before Fatbar and I decided to run away, she'd came home early from work and caught me in his room. That woman hated my black ass. She told me I would never be happy, that as soon as I thought I was, a black cloud would come and take all my happiness away. Same as I had done to her." Harlin hung her head low as tears fell from her eyes.

"Mama, you are not a black cloud, and none of your happiness is being taken away. Daddy is going to be fine."

"Look at me, sitting here putting my problems on you when you have your own shit going on. I'm sorry baby," Harlin stated, standing from her seat and wiping her tears. "How is Nakia? Is there any word on the baby?" she continued.

"Nakia is okay, and the baby is stable. We're just waiting on them to let us see him. Nakia said we have to see him before we can give him a name."

"Yeah, I know exactly what you mean. We didn't even have a name for you or your sister my entire pregnancy, but as soon as y'all came out, the names came right to us. Has Rosa gotten here yet?"

"Yeah, she's in the waiting room. She doesn't want to see pops until he's awake and can talk to her," Raphael informed.

Harlin nodded her head, already knowing how her daughter was. She hated hospitals, so the fact she was even in the waiting room said a lot. Harlin prayed that everything would indeed be fine and Fatbar would be okay just like the doctors said; however, she was more worried about what caused the heart attack. She knew he'd been on the phone just moments prior, and she couldn't help but wonder if the phone call had anything to do with it.

"I'm about to go talk to the doctor and see if they know what time Nakia and I can see the baby. I'll come back later and check on y'all," Raphael said before hugging his mother and walking out the room.

"Yes, soon as your fiancé gets back, you two can go see your new baby boy," Raphael heard the doctor say as he entered the room. "And it looks like that's now," the doctor continued. "I'm just gonna go get a wheelchair for you, Nakia, and I'll be right back."

Nakia smiled as she nodded her head. She was extremely excited to be meeting her baby for the first time and couldn't wait to hold him. She looked over at Raphael and could tell he was feeling the same joy she was. Within moments, Doctor Sutton was back, and Nakia and Raphael were on their way to meet their new bundle of joy.

Once in the NICU, they were brought over to an incubator with two small holes on each side. The tag on the incubator read "Baby Pitchford" and Nakia knew it was her son. Inside the incubator, however, was the tiniest baby Nakia had ever seen. He had tubes in his mouth and nose, as well as a heart monitor stuck to his chest. Nakia's heart broke at the sight, as she wished she could have kept her baby inside her until the full-term of her pregnancy.

"Why is there so many tubes?" Raphael asked.

"Well, the lungs are one of the last organs that become fully developed for a fetus, so the tube coming from his nose is what's breathing for him. He will have that until he is able to breathe on his own. The tube in his mouth is a feeding tube, and everything else is monitoring his heart," Doctor Sutton informed.

Raphael nodded his head slowly in understanding as he placed his hand on Nakia's shoulder. He wasn't prepared to see his son like this, and he wanted to break down in tears. However, he knew he had to be strong for Nakia.

"How much does he weigh?" Nakia asked.

"He was two pounds and six ounces when he was born, which is bout average for a baby born at thirty weeks," the doctor answered. "Would you like to hold him?" She continued.

Raphael and Nakia took turns holding their baby in their arms. He was so small that Raphael was almost too afraid to hold him. However, once he did, he vowed to him that he would protect him with his life.

"I think we should name him Aden, what do you think about that?" Raphael asked.

"I think Aden is perfect." Nakia smiled.

Once back in her hospital room, Nakia was finally able to breathe a little easier. She had needed that visit with her son, to meet with him and let him know he wasn't alone. She couldn't wait until the day when they were both out the hospital and at home with the rest of their family. She couldn't wait to introduce Aden to Rashaud and Lexi because Nakia knew they would be wonderful siblings to their new little brother.

CHAPTER FIVE

Tianna had been working all day with one thing on her mind, and that was her meeting with Darden. She prayed he would allow her to break out with them because she had to leave. There was no way she could stay in Albania any longer. She needed to get her freedom back and she needed to be back home. She missed her life she had, the one before she met Russell. She was happy with the life she had, and if it wasn't for Russell coming in and fucking it all up, she wouldn't be in the situation she was in now. She hated what she'd let him do to her and needed to fix it.

Once Tianna was done with her last client of the day, she went to take a shower before heading to her room. She didn't know what time Darden would be coming to talk to her, but she would wait up until he came. A few hours after Tianna got done eating her dinner, she heard a faint knock on her door. Getting up from her bed, she went and answered it. Just as expected, Darden and Tiny were standing on the other side. Smiling, she let them both in and closed the door behind them.

"Hey Tianna, this is Darden; Darden, this is Tianna," Tiny introduced.

Darden smiled before shaking Tianna's hand. "Yes, I see her around here all the time, but this is the first time we are officially meeting. It's nice to meet you, Tianna."

"Thank you, it's nice to meet you as well."

"Darden, Tianna is one of the few friends I have here, and I want her to come with us. She deserves to leave just as much as we do," Tiny stated.

"Baby, as long as you trust her, then it's all good," Darden spoke in his thick Albanian ascent.

"So, I can come with y'all, just like that?" Tianna asked.

"Yes, if my baby say you good people, then you good people. You just gotta be ready to leave tomorrow night because that's when we making our move," Darden answered.

Hell, Tianna would have been ready if he would have said they were leaving tonight. She wanted out of that place as fast as she could, and if tomorrow was the fastest, then she would take it. She sat on her bed, as Darden laid out their escape plan to her.

They would leave at night while everyone was sleeping. There was a door in the basement of the building that would lead them out the back way into a wooded area. That way, the guards wouldn't be able to see them. They would travel through the woods until they came to an old, abandoned warehouse, where they would stay until it was time to board the ship that would take them into America. Feeling confident, Tianna agreed to be ready when Darden and Tiny came to get her the following night. For the first time in over a year, Tianna went to sleep hopeful.

That next morning when she woke up, she went right to the bathroom to shower and start her day. She was eager for tonight and knew all she had to do was get through this one last day. After showering, Tianna slicked her hair back before dressing in a red bustier and matching boy shorts. No sooner than she got back to her room, Agon barged through her door, letting her know it was time for her first client. He looked at her, confused about her maintained appearance. He'd never seen Tianna look this well-groomed before, and he had to admit he was getting turned on. He licked his lips and his eyes roamed her body. He had to catch himself because he knew she had a job to do.

"Let's go, we don't want to keep your client waiting," Agon spoke.

Without hesitation, Tianna walked out the room with Agon leading the way. She smiled and held her head high as she took the walk down the hallway, knowing this was one of the last times she would be taking that walk. Tianna didn't even need a high from whatever drug they were offering; she was high off life knowing hers could only get better from here. She walked into the room ready to service her client.

Around six that evening, Tianna was twelve clients in and had just gotten out of the shower for the fourth time that day. Her clients had been coming so fast that she hadn't had time to shower in-between all of them. She'd just finished putting lotion on her body and was just about to get dressed when Agon walked into her room.

"Damn, do I have another client already? Okay, let me just slip my clothes on right quick," Tianna stated, quickly trying to slip on the pair of tiny black leather shorts she had in her hand.

Agon didn't say a word, just closed the door. He walked closer to Tianna, and she turned around to face him.

"I'm coming right now Agon, just let me put my top on."

Agon still didn't utter a word as he walked up so close to Tianna, she could smell the liquor on his breath. She moved to take a step back when he grabbed her arm roughly. With his free hand, he cupped Tianna's bare breasts, twirling her nipples between his two fingers. Tianna tensed up, confused about what was going on.

"A-Agon, what are you doing?" Tianna asked as she tried to pull away from his grasp.

"You give that shit to everybody else, it's time I tasted some of them sweet juices too," he replied.

With those words, Tianna's eyes widened as her heart began beating rapidly. She tried her best to get away from Agon, but his grip was too tight. Grabbing her face roughly, Agon placed a sloppy wet kiss on Tianna's lips. The smell of his breath almost made her pass out. Agon had never did anything like this before, so the entire situation was catching Tianna off guard.

"Agon, please, you don't have to do this," Tianna pleaded.

"Shut the fuck up and get down on your knees; I want some of that strong dick sucking that all your clients talk about," Agon insisted as he began pushing Tianna to the floor.

Tianna couldn't believe this was happening. In all the time she'd been there, the only men who had ever touched her had been her clients. Now, there she was, on her knees staring up at Agon's huge frame. In the time it took him to let her go so he could unzip his pants, Tianna had made it to her feet and attempted to run to her bedroom door. However, she was too slow. Agon grabbed her, tossing her like a rag doll onto her bed. Tianna screamed out in an effort to get someone to come into her room and stop him; however, her screams fell on deaf ears because nobody came.

Agon laid on top of Tianna, damn near smothering her small frame as he roughly sucked on her nipples. She jerked and squirmed as though she was having a seizure as she tried to get him off of her. Sick of her moving, Agon slapped Tianna so hard, she could see stars.

"No, shut the fuck up! You taking all the enjoyment out of this with all that fucking screaming you doing!" Agon yelled.

Ripping off Tianna's leather shorts Agon forcefully opened her legs. She fought and yelled, but nothing she did stopped him from entering her. Agon pumped in and out of her as he grunted and growled like a bear, as Tianna laid motionless underneath him with tears streaming down her face.

"Yeah, you stopped fighting it; now, this shit feels good," Agon panted.

Tianna didn't say a word as she laid there getting violated in the worse way. The five minutes Agon took to nut felt like forever in Tianna's eyes, as she prayed for it to be over quickly. Agon made one last thrust into Tianna's vagina before pulling his wet manhood from inside her. He breathed heavily as he sat naked in the edge of her bed.

"That shit was good as hell. I see why the clients ask for you so much," he spoke.

Tianna just laid there looking up at the ceiling with tears streaming down her cheeks. She couldn't understand why this was happening to her. The disgust she felt was immeasurable. A thousand showers couldn't wash away the filth she felt inside her. Why was this happening to her? All she wanted was a better life, one she could be proud to say was her own. The dreams she had were all about to come true, only to now be fucked away in Albania. Turning her head to the side, she saw the leather shorts that Agon had just ripped off of her like paper.

"I'ma need that shit again, but right now, you need to get washed up for your next client," Agon stated.

Tianna just couldn't take it anymore. With those words, she grabbed her shorts, wrapped the torn ends around both her hands and cloaked them around Agon's neck, choking him. His big frame was nothing against the anger she felt, as Agon attempted to fight back. Tianna placed her leg around his neck, adding extra force. Agon clawed at Tianna's legs in an effort to break free, but she felt nothing. Her adrenaline was through the roof and all she knew was if she didn't kill him, then he would kill her, and she wasn't going for that.

The compression Tianna was applying to Agon's neck was cutting off his air supply and making it harder for him to fight back. He hit her thighs weakly as he tried to fight off losing consciousness. Tianna, however, wasn't letting up until she knew he was dead, even choking him several more seconds longer than she needed to, just to assure he wouldn't breathe again.

"Fuck, fuck, fuck. What the hell did I just do?" Tianna whispered to herself as she realized that she would be dead anyway once they found Agon in her room.

Tianna paced her floor with her hand on her chin, trying to figure out her next move. With no other options, Tianna used all the strength she had to move Agon's dead weight from on her bed to under it. Her heart pounded as she hurriedly dressed and slipped into a pair of shoes. Tianna cautiously opened her room door, looking both to the right and left before she exited, closing the door behind her. She quickly walked through the hallways, looking behind her every few steps to make sure nobody was behind her. Once she got to Tiny's room, she opened the door and walked inside, startling Tiny, who was sitting on her bed.

"Bitch, you scared the hell outta me. What's wrong with you? Why you running in here like that?" Tiny asked.

"Tiny, we gotta leave like right now; we can't wait until everybody goes to sleep. We gotta go now! We need to find Darden," Tianna announced.

Tiny looked at Tianna, confused as to what she was talking about. They already had a plan with a time to leave, and she couldn't understand why she wanted to defer from that. Standing to her feet, Tiny walked over to Tianna, looking deep into her eyes, waiting for her to tell her what was up. She could tell by the scared look on her face that something happened, and she needed to know what that was.

"I killed Agon," Tianna whispered, looking over her shoulder as if someone other than them was in the room.

Tiny's eyes widened and her bottom lip dropped. She couldn't believe what she'd just heard and knew once someone found out, all hell would break loose.

"What the fuck do you mean you killed him? Why the hell would you do that Tianna? We were on our way out of here in just a few short hours," Tiny spoke, trying to understand her friend's logic behind her actions.

"He raped me," Tianna said weakly. She dropped her head low, but Tiny could still see the tears that fell from her eyes.

Sympathetically, Tiny hugged her friend. She could feel the hurt coming from Tianna and knew that if she was in that situation, she would have done the same thing. Her heart went out to Tianna, and she knew they would now have to leave before the shit hit the fan. Once they knew Agon was dead, the entire place would be on lockdown.

"Where is his body at right now?" Tiny asked.

"In my room, under my bed."

"Are you sure he's dead?"

"Yeah, he's definitely dead. I choked the shit out of him," Tianna replied.

Tiny nodded her head as she tried to think about what they would do next. It was still too early in the evening for them to leave. It was still daylight, and the staff and security were still on high alert. She needed to speak with Darden and let him know what happened, hoping he would have a temporary solution, at least until they could get outside the brothel. Going over to her bed, she lifted her mattress and pulled out a cell phone, calling Darden and asking him to come to her room as soon as possible.

The two waited in silence for what seemed like forever until Darden was finally able to get to them. He walked into the room walking directly to Tiny and asked her if she was okay. When she replied yes, he asked what was going on. Darden knew for Tiny to call him before she was finished with all her clients for the day meant that something must be going on.

"Tianna killed Agon. He raped her, and now, he's in her room dead. We need to get out of here before they find out he's gone," Tiny announced.

Darden just stared at Tiny in shock, completely taken aback by what he'd just been told. They were supposed to be running; killing was never in their plan. Darden shook his head, not wanting to get in the middle of Tianna's mess. This had nothing to do with him or Tiny. This was Tianna's problem and she would have to handle it. This was why he'd wished Tiny never told Tianna about their plan to leave because now, the company had thrown a curve ball and added extra heat on them.

"We can't leave now, it's too hot. All eyes are still open, which means they'll be on us. We can't get out of here like that. We'll definitely be caught. And why do we have to leave now? She killed Agon, not us," Darden stated.

Tiny cut her eyes at him, as if she couldn't believe he would leave her friend out here like that. They all knew what would happen to Tianna if anyone found out she killed Agon, and Tiny wasn't gonna let that happen. She knew that Darden knew this entire building like the back of his hand so, if anyone could get them out of it alive, it was him. Tiny knew he was serious about not wanting to be involved in Agon's murder, and he wasn't; hell, neither was she. However, she also knew there was no way she was gonna leave her friend out to dry, so she played the one card she had that would get Darden on board.

"We have to leave now, Darden. Once they find out about Agon, this entire place will be on lockdown and we will be unable to leave. That ship leaves tomorrow, and if we not on it, we never getting back to America. We can't raise our baby in a place like this Darden; we can't even be a family here," Tiny informed, rubbing on her stomach.

Darden looked at her, knowing what she just said was true. If they couldn't get on that ship, then it would be over. They would be stuck in Albania for God knows how long, and Darden couldn't have that. So, against his better judgment, he agreed to leave now.

"I'll be back in fifteen minutes, and we can leave then."

Tiny nodded her head, and Darden walked out the door. She threw on a pair of pants and a shirt and waited on Darden to return. Both Tiny and Tianna were nervous, as their hearts beat fast inside their chests. Tiny quickly slipped into a pair of pants and a shirt before sliding into get sneakers. They waited for what seemed like forever for Darden to return, and once he did, they were ready to go.

Cautiously, the three of them walked out of Tiny's room, looking from right to left and behind them as they walked through the halls. Darden walked in front of them as he led the way. He motioned them down a set of stairs before they came to a set of metal double doors. Darden peeked in the small glass window in the center of the metal door to make sure no one was on the other side. When he didn't see anyone, he used one of the keys from the huge key ring that hung from his pants and opened the door. The three of them quickly walked through it and raced down the hall to another set of stairs.

"Okay, now, these stairs will lead us to the basement and the way out. There will be several armed guards outside, so we have to be quick and stay close by me, so you won't get lost. Once we are in the woods, we should be good, but the hard part is going to be getting past the guards to get there," Darden informed.

The two ladies nodded their heads in understanding before Darden led them down the stairs. Tianna's hands shook with each step she took downward, not knowing what she was walking into. Darden was the only one of them with a weapon, a gun that he had tucked away in his waistline. So, if something did pop off, he would be the only one shooting for the three of them. Making their way to the door, Darden spotted one of the guards walking towards it. Thinking quick on his feet, he turned around and placed his finger on his lips, informing the woman to be quiet as he motioned them to stand against the wall.

Darden watched silently as the guard unknowingly walked into his own death. Darden pulled a small knife from his pocket and clutched the handle in his fist tightly, as he awaited the guard. As soon as the guard opened the door, Darden was on him, catching him off guard and stabbing him directly in the neck, putting him down instantly. Both Tiny and Tianna watched on in horror, as Darden killed the man with no remorse. Darden dragged the man over to the other side of the basement and out of view.

When he returned, the three of them made their way out the door and into the scorching Albanian heat. Even though it was after six in the evening, the sun was still beaming, causing it to be a hundred degrees outside. Darden pulled the gun from his waistline and held it at his side, as he led the way around the building. Tianna and Tiny were his extra eyes, as they watched for any potential threats. Darden saw two guards standing at their posts with their backs facing them and pointed them out to the ladies.

Staying as quiet as they could, they kept walking until they got around to a pathway that led to the wooded area Darden spoke about. The three of them ran top speed through the woods, and even though Tianna was out of breath and hot, she kept running. Afraid that if she stopped, they would all be caught. Making it out the brothel was one thing; however, they still had hours to go before the ship was scheduled to depart the next morning. So, with that, they all knew they had to stay out of eyesight of anyone affiliated with the group that owned the brothel. A sense of relief came over all three of them once they got to the doors of the abandoned warehouse.

CHAPTER SIX

Nikki laid in bed watching TV as she waited on Cole to return with their food. He'd left several hours ago, and Nikki felt her best when he was gone. She wanted to tell him that she didn't want to be with him, but she felt that it might backfire on her. So, for now, she would have to keep her mouth shut. Nikki's stomach growled and she rubbed it, trying to ease her hunger pains. She'd waited on him as long as she could, but the hunger was becoming too much for her.

Getting up from her bed, she went in the kitchen in search of something quick to eat. Cole had been gone for hours, and although she wanted to wait on him, she wasn't gonna starve herself. Looking through the fridge, Nikki found everything she needed to make herself a turkey sandwich. Once she was done, she grabbed a bottled water and some chips before heading back to her room.

Nikki had just taken the second bite of her sandwich when Cole finally came in with the food she was supposed to have hours ago. He stumbled into the room, and Nikki could tell he was drunk. She didn't say anything, just rolled her eyes and continued to eat her sandwich.

"What up doooee? I got us sooome orange chicken and.... yooooo, why is yooou eatin' when you know I went to get food?" Cole asked, slurring his words drunkenly.

Nikki didn't say a word, just continued to eat. She looked up at him, disgusted by his drunken state. She'd seen Cole get sloppy drunk a few times over the weeks they'd been hanging out and she hated how he acted. He was always so loud and irate. One time, he almost got her kicked out of her motel room for all the noise. Nikki didn't want to have a repeat of that same incident, so she kept quiet, not wanting to trigger him in any way.

"Bitch, I know you hear me talkin' to you! Why the fuck are you eatin'? You made me waste my money on this food that yo ass ain't even gonna eat?" Cole yelled, his deep baritone invading Nikki's ears.

She looked up at him with her nose turned up at the mention of him calling her out her name. He'd never done that before, and Nikki knew Cole had to have been extremely drunk for him to do something so stupid. Still trying to keep her cool, Nikki took a deep breath before she responded.

"Look Cole, I know you drunk or whateva, but don't be callin' me out my name. That shit ain't cool and calm down before the neighbors hear you. Why you so loud?"

Nikki placed her plate on the nightstand and continued, "I'm eatin' because I waited on you for hours to come back, and I got hungry. What was I supposed to do, not eat?"

Rage shot through Cole like a bolt of lightning. *Who the fuck does this bitch thinks she's talking to?* Cole thought to himself as he stood there eyeing Nikki. He walked over to her, sitting the bag of food on the nightstand next to her plate. Cole opened the bag and pulled out one of the white foam containers and opened it. Without warning, Cole poured the contents all over Nikki's head before smashing the container in her face. Nikki quickly snatched his hand away from her face, as orange chicken sauce dripped down her head and into her eyes.

"Man, what the fuck is wrong with you? Why the fuck would you—"

SLAP!

Before Nikki could even finish her sentence, Cole hit her across he face so hard, it sent her falling backwards on the bed. Shocked, she grabbed her face and looked up at Cole, confused. He'd never hit her before, so Nikki was caught off guard, not knowing what to do. She couldn't even speak as she held the side of her face and stared up at Cole.

"Bitch, who the fuck you think you talking to? You think you can just sit there and get out of pocket with me? Oh, bitch, I'ma show you what it is! You got me fucked up!" Cole yelled before jumping onto the bed, straddling Nikki. He threw blow after blow, hitting Nikki in her face and chest. Cole didn't give a damn where the hits landed, as long as they connected.

Nikki screamed for Cole to stop as she tried to shield her face from the beating he was giving her. She tried to move, but the weight of his body on top of her kept her in place. She kicked and screamed, but no matter what she did, Cole continued to throw punches. Nikki cried out loud as she silently prayed for Cole to stop hitting her. The force of his blows had Nikki's head spinning, and she knew she would have major damage whenever he decided to stop.

Out of breath, Cole finally fell over on the bed alongside Nikki. Still crying, Nikki jumped up and ran into the bathroom, locking the door behind her. Sliding onto the floor, she wept uncontrollably. Why was this her life? She was only seventeen and had been through more things than some women twice her age. Nikki couldn't do a thing except hold her head down and cry. There was no way she was gonna let Cole beat on her at his convenience. She didn't leave Russell just to be mistreated by Cole.

With that, Nikki found her strength. Getting up from the floor, she used the bathroom tissue to wipe her face before walking out of the bathroom. Cole was no longer in the room; instead, he was in the living room sitting on the couch. Nikki walked pass him without saying a word. Walking into the kitchen, she grabbed a black Hefty bag and headed back to the bedroom. Going through all the drawers, she put everything that belonged to Cole inside, even grabbing his toiletries and placing them in the bag as well.

Walking back into the living room, bag in hand, Nikki threw it at Cole's feet before telling him to get out. She didn't care what she would have to do to make sure her bills were paid; she was going to do it on her own. There was no way she would let Cole beat on her. She'd just got out of a situation where she was someone's door mat and punching bag, she'd be damned if she did it again.

"Get out of what, my house?" Cole stated nonchalantly.

Sitting up from the couch and folding his arms in front of him, Cole looked up at Nikki, smiling. The beating he'd given her had sobered him up a bit, making him more aware of what was going on. He knew he had the upper hand. His name was on everything, so he knew Nikki didn't hold any weight there. The mere thought she had that she did was what made the situation comical to Cole.

"Where is your name at on any of the paperwork Nikki? You not even on the lease, so what you talkin' bout? I'm not going nowhere. If I leave, you won't have a place to stay. And I'm sure we both know that. Yo ass would be on the streets with nothing just like when I found you. If you wanna go back to that, then that's on you. I'ma be good either way," Cole spoke. His no-nonsense tone broke Nikki with each word.

"This is my house Cole," Nikki spoke weakly. "You got it for me. You don't have to pay any more of the bills. I will take over from here on out. You not taking my house from me, though. And you not stayin' with me. Look at what you did to my face Cole." Nikki stood firm no matter how much she shook inside, as she pointed to her busted lip and swollen face.

"See, that's the thing, this ain't your house. It's mine, and I ain't going nowhere and neither are you, so take my stuff back in the room and put it away."

Nikki looked on in defeat, knowing Cole was right. His name wasn't on everything so, legally, she had no claim to the house. Cole had her exactly where he wanted her, and there was nothing she could do about it. With tears in her eyes, she grabbed the bag and went to put Cole's belongings away.

———

Nakia laid in her hospital bed eating ice chips and watching the news. She wanted to know if the police had found the body in her home, but she had yet to see a report. No officers had even come up to question

THE STATE'S WITNESS 2

her, and she didn't understand why. She told Raphael they needed to call the police, and although he was reluctant, Nakia was sure he'd done the right thing. However, if he'd done so, why wasn't anyone there?

"I'm gonna run home, shower and change clothes. Do you want me to bring you something from the house?" Raphael asked, walking into Nakia's room.

"Yeah, I need my purse, phone and charger. I also need some clothes to come home in. Matter fact, bring my hospital bag; it has clothes for me and the baby inside," Nakia answered.

Nodding his head, Raphael walked over to her, kissing her on the forehead before telling her he would be back. He didn't want to leave her, but he knew Jalyn would make sure she was good. In actuality, he wanted to go back to the house and make sure any damage caused by the intruder was indeed cleaned up. The last thing he wanted was for Nakia to come home and see anything from that night. Before leaving the hospital, Raphael stopped in to let his mother know the same. He offered to bring her back some food, but she declined. Knowing he would bring her something back anyway, he nodded his head before closing the door.

Raphael walked into his home and immediately smelled the rotten food Nakia had brought home the night it all happened. After throwing it out, Raphael searched the house to find out how the intruder entered. Investigating every inch of the first floor of the home, he finally found the unlocked window. Shaking his head at the near fatal mistake, Raphael locked the window before heading up the stairs to shower. He saw the blood at the top of the stairs and couldn't believe Manny didn't clean it up. There was no way he missed a puddle of blood in the middle of the floor. Once Raphael had cleaned the blood up himself, he was ready to take his shower.

Raphael's eyes widened once he walked into their ensuite bathroom and saw the crime scene. Although there was no body, the amount of blood and broken glass made it evident a murder had occurred. Thinking that Manny had not had a chance to clean up, Raphael went into the guest bathroom to shower. He knew he would have to come back the next day to assure everything was to his liking. He also was going to put more cameras up and a new security system. Raphael wanted Nakia to feel safe in their home and he would do anything to make sure she did.

After stopping at Panera and grabbing a few sandwiches, Raphael made his way back to the hospital, stopping in to see Nakia before he went to his father's room. After giving Nakia the items she'd requested, he headed to his father's room, sandwiches in hand. Once inside, he saw his father up and talking. Raphael smiled at the fact that he was started to sound like himself again.

"What up, Pops? I see you in here looking good," Raphael stated.

"Yeah, I'm starting to feel a little better. Ain't no small ass heart attack gonna hold me down, you know I'm a G," Fatbar announced.

"Your father seems to think he needs to get right back to business as usual, instead of giving his body time to heal. He's clearly under a lot of stress and I'm telling him he needs to take a break, but he won't listen to me. Raphael, please talk to your father because I can't go through this again," Harlin stated as she walked out the room. Raphael could tell that her nerves was getting the best of her.

Raphael took a seat next to Fatbar, not knowing what to say. He knew his mother was scared and he didn't want that. At the same time, however, he knew what a hardworking man his father was. He built his business from the ground up, so to just tell him to take a step back would be close to impossible. He opened his mouth to speak, but before he could utter a word, Fatbar beat him to it.

"The man Nakia killed was Niko," he spoke.

Raphael's mouth dropped open in disbelief. He looked over at him, hoping his father was going to tell him he was joking. How the fuck was his cousin dead, and more importantly, how was his soon to be wife the murderer? What the fuck was really going on? He didn't even have time to ask questions as his father continued.

"Nakia is the witness in Russell's case. I had no clue it was her when I sent Niko on the job. Russell did give me the names and addresses, however, I never looked at them. I didn't know any of this until Manny called me once he got to your house and saw who it was."

Raphael placed his hands over his head as he tried to process his father's words. These last few days had been hell for him, and it was doing nothing but getting worse. The fact that Manny knew what had gone down was cause enough for worry. His mind went straight into protective mode, knowing he would have to protect Nakia from Manny's supreme murder game.

"Did you know Nakia had been called in to testify?" Fatbar asked.

Raphael shook his head no, as he wondered why Nakia hadn't told him. *Damn, I was about to kill her co-worker that night,* Raphael thought. His mind was running wild, and this was all too much for him. Before they could finish the conversation, Harlin walked in, stopping their talk.

———

Nakia had seven voicemails and fourteen text messages when she charged her phone. Most of them were from Bailey and Anastasia, but a couple were from her children. They wanted to know when they could come home and why Nakia wasn't answering her phone. The planned weekend slumber party had turned into days without her seeing her kids. She knew she needed to call Bailey and Anastasia back because the urgency in their voice let her know something had happened, and after what happened to her, she could only imagine what that was. She'd just got to the last voicemail when her entire demeanor changed. It was the detective assigned to the case, letting Nakia know they had set a trial date, and she must contact him. Rolling her eyes, Nakia called her children to let them know she'd given birth to their brother. Rashaud and Lexi were both so happy to hear the news and couldn't wait to meet him.

"Y'all have to stay with Auntie Simone for a few more day til I am released from the hospital; then, y'all can come home," she stated, hating that she would have to spend more days without her children. This was the longest they'd been without each other since Nakia had given birth to them, and the separation was killing her. It had been just the three of them for so long that it felt weird to be without them for just a day, let alone an entire week.

Shaking off that sadness she felt, Nakia dialed Bailey. The phone rang three times before she picked it up.

"Girl, I've been calling you and calling you; are you okay?" Bailey asked.

"I am now, it's been a lot going on."

"Tell me about it. I've been staying at Anastasia's house. I'm scared to go home; that man sent someone to my house the other day and almost killed me. If I would have been inside, I know I would have been dead. Thankfully, I was pulling into the parking lot when I saw him lurking around my apartment. Girl, he shot at me and followed me all the way to the police station. I was so scared," Bailey confirmed.

Nakia went on to tell Bailey everything that happened to her that same night, and they both were in disbelief by the end of the conversation. They vowed to each other not to testify in the case and would just not answer any more of the agent's calls. They both thought if they just ignored him, he would go away.

CHAPTER SEVEN

Tianna and Tiny followed Darden through the building, as they searched for a safe place for them to camp out. Thankfully, it was still daylight outside, and they used the sunlight to guide their way through the building. Once the sun went down, they would have no means of light. They couldn't start a fire because the light coming from it would most definitely get them caught. Tianna knew that by now, someone had to have found Agon's body in her room and could only imagine what was going on back at the brothel. She knew that they had to be looking for her, and once they didn't find her inside the brothel, there would be a BOLO out for her within moments. The shooters the brothel had were ruthless so, Tianna knew if they were found, there would be no escaping them.

Even though she was with Tiny and Darden, Tianna knew she was on her own. Darden wouldn't protect her the way he would protect Tiny, and Tianna knew that. If anything popped off, Tianna knew that she would be responsible for her own protection, so she was gonna stay alert at all times. She would feel a lot better once she got on the ship and it set sail. Once they were in a part of the building that Darden felt was secure, they set up for the night. Darden took watch as he let Tianna and Tiny get some rest. Although he was tired, his nerves were on edge and fear of being caught plagued him. If anyone did come looking for them, Darden was going to make sure he spotted them first.

Darden jumped up the next morning, terrified that he'd fallen asleep. He prayed they hadn't missed the ship. Looking down at his watch, he saw they only had an hour to get there. After waking both Tianna and Tiny, the three cautiously left the building, looking over their shoulders with every few steps. Darden knew they would have to be extra careful because all the guards were on duty in the morning. He knew that, by now, they all knew the three of them were gone and that Agon was dead. He could only imagine the amount of people that was looking for them and the fire power that came with them.

Darden was afraid; however, he didn't want to show it. He didn't want Tiny to see his fear because he wanted her to know he would do anything to protect her and their unborn child. He would lay down his life for the two of them, and although he was praying that wouldn't have to happen, he wouldn't think twice if it did. He loved Tiny and wanted her to know she would be safe with him.

The three moved swiftly through the woods as they approached a main road. Darden turned to the women and explained to them that they would have to cross it. Letting them know this was the main road the guards traveled to and from the brothel, he informed them that they had to stay on high alert in order to not be seen. Darden looked both ways down the road to make sure he didn't see a car coming. Once he was certain the coast was clear, he told them it was okay to cross. With Tianna going first, she placed her foot on the pavement and immediately heard gun shots from behind them. Knowing it was guards from the brothel, her heart dropped to her stomach as fear set in.

"Run!" Darden yelled as he realized they'd been spotted. His heart beat rapidly and he could only pray they would make it to the ship before any of them got hurt. The three of them ran at top speed as shots flew into their direction.

"Ahhh!" Tiny screamed as a bullet flew right past her head, only missing it by a few inches.

"Come on, we gotta move faster," Darden stated, looking back and seeing four men just a few feet behind them.

"Stop where you are!" One of the guards yelled out to them. The words fell on deaf ears because none of them stopped, knowing that if they did, they would surely be killed.

Tianna ran at top speed, not even taking the time to look back. She didn't know where she was going but she knew she need to get the fuck away from the dudes that were shooting at them. She knew if she was caught, she was dead and she'd came way too far to let that happen. She heard Darden yell to turn left, and she did just that. She was tired and out of breath, but she kept running. The four men continued to call out for them to stop, and they let go round after round in their direction.

Pow! Pow! Pow! The shots rang out, but the three of them never looked back. It didn't matter how close the guards were, all that was on their minds was to keep running forward. Knowing that once they made it to the ship, it wouldn't be anything the guards could do. It would be too many people around, and the one thing they didn't want to do was draw any unwanted attention to the brothel. Getting on a ship with guns in hand would do just that.

Darden felt a little relief as he saw the ship in the distance. He knew they were close, a few hundred feet at most, and once they were on the ship, it wouldn't be anything the shooters could do. The hard part was them getting there unharmed. With all the shots coming in their direction, it would be a miracle if they made it without being gunned down first.

"Speed up, we don't have far to go, just straight ahead!" Darden yelled.

"I will kill you! Stop fucking running!" Another guard yelled in his thick Albanian accent. His voice sent chills up Tianna's spine, and she knew they needed to hurry and get to the ship.

"Come on Tiny, run baby, just keep running straight," Darden coached.

The words had just left his mouth when the most excruciating pain he'd ever felt burned through his shoulder and down his arm. He grabbed it on instinct, gripping it while trying to ease the pain. The wetness on his hand let him know what happened, as he bit his bottom lip in an attempt to tolerate the pain. He'd been shot. A bullet had pierced his flesh, sending shooting pain throughout his entire arm. He wanted to scream out in pain, but before he could, Tiny began to scream, as he watched her fall to the ground. Thinking of nothing but Tiny's safety, Darden quickly ran over to her, trying to help her to her feet. She'd tripped over a branch and twisted her ankle, making it almost impossible for her to stand on it.

Tianna, who was still running, refused to look back to see what was causing all the screaming out of fear it might slow her down. She could still hear the guns being fired, so she knew the guards were still on their toes. She heard Darden calling out to her, asking for her help, and she froze. Tianna didn't know what to do; everything in her wanted to keep running, to not stop til she made it to the ship. She knew she needed to get to the ship and she was afraid that if she stopped running, she would be caught. On the other hand, she knew she wouldn't have even made it out the brothel if it wasn't for Tiny and Darden. So, even though it took everything Tianna had in her, she turned around and ran back to help them.

"Please help her, she fell and can't walk. I'll hold these muthafuckas off as long as I can," Darden exclaimed, pulling the one gun he had from his waistline. Darden was outnumbered and he knew it. He was only one person with eight bullets, so he knew he was no match for the four men and their ammo. However, if it meant Tiny would have a chance to make it onto the ship and sail away to freedom, he knew he would have to try.

Tianna took Tiny's arm, placed it over her shoulder, and wrapped her arm around Tiny's waist. She told Tiny to lean all of her weight against her and to move as fast as she could. Tiny nodded her head in understanding, and the two of them moved as fast as they could towards the ship. They could hear the shots behind them, but they were too focused on making it to their destination to think about anything happening behind them.

Tianna could hear the horns of the ship blaring and knew her freedom was close. Her and Tiny were almost at the dock, and Darden wasn't too far behind them. One of the guards had already met their demise by the hands of Darden. A single shot to the head sent the man to the ground, unable to ever get back up again. Darden would take down as many of them as he could because there was no way he was going down without a fight. He was relieved once they'd all made it to the dock.

"Help her get on the ship; my cousin is waiting for us. He will tell y'all where to go from there," Darden stated.

"Wait, where are you going? Come with us Darden," Tiny cried, confused about what was going on.

"I'll be right behind you; I just want to make sure the guards don't come to the dock. Once I see y'all on the ship, I'll get on," Darden said.

Tiny shook her head with tear-filled eyes. She didn't understand why Darden wouldn't just get on the ship with them. There was no reason for him to stay behind until they got on. Tiny pleaded with him to rethink his decision. Tianna, who saw the men getting closer to the dock, yelled out to Tiny to come on. Darden quickly turned in the direction of the guards with his gun drawn. However, before he could pull the trigger, a shot was fired, tearing through his chest, causing him to hit the ground with a huge thud. Tianna instantly knew he was gone as soon as his body hit the ground.

Tiny screamed out loud, falling to her knees alongside Darden's lifeless body as she begged him to get up. She didn't care about the guards that were only a few feet away from them. Her heart had just been ripped out of her chest and stomped on before being discarded in the trash. Darden was just talking to her, telling her he would be right behind them. Now, within seconds, his soul had left his body as he transitioned into the next form of life.

"Tiny, get up! We gotta get on this ship before they have both of us laying here, too."

Tianna didn't mean to come off insensitive, but she needed Tiny to snap out of whatever trance she was in and get on the ship with her. They'd come so far, and she would be damned if they didn't both get on this ship and get out of this bullshit together. Tiny, still weeping uncontrollably, held her hand out for Tianna to help her up. She did so, and the two women moved as fast as they could onto the ship.

———

Russell woke up to the thunder blaring, scaring him out of his sleep. His little feet hit the floor and he grabbed his teddy bear, cradling it in his arms. The thunder was so loud, it had little Russell trembling. He called out for his mom, and when she didn't answer, he thought she was unable to hear him over the loud rumbling. Letting his little feet move through the room, he opened his bedroom door and walked down the hallway towards his mother's room. Once he got to her closed bedroom door, he turned the knob and attempted to enter.

"Yo, what you doing lil homie? Don't you know that when you come to a closed door, you supposed to knock? Somebody needs to teach yo lil ass some fuckin manners!" The deep baritone blared, startling Russell.

Russell jumped, not expecting the man to be in his mother's room. He'd never seen this man before and didn't know who he was. His mother had never let any other man come around him or his brother since their father had walked out on them in the middle of the night over two years ago. She'd told both Russell and Travis that their father would come back; he just needed some time away. Although she still prayed every night for his safe return, deep down, she knew he was never coming back. The family life and responsibility of taking care of everyone had become too much for him. His mental state had been tampered with, and it was almost impossible for him to remain sane. Unable to see another way out, he left his girlfriend to fend for their young sons on her own.

"Mommy, you in here?" Russell called out, ignoring the man, and walking past him. Russell saw his mother sprawled across her bed in an oversized t-shirt and socks.

"What's wrong baby?" Rochelle cooed as she sat up in her bed.

"Mommy, I'm scared. The thunder is too loud. Can I sleep in here with you?"

"Sure baby, come on up here with mommy," Rochelle replied.

Smiling, Russell used his little feet to run towards his mother as fast as he could. He loved his mother with all his heart. She would do anything she could to make sure he and his brother were good. She gave them all the love in the world, and Russell always felt safe whenever his mother was around. In his eyes, she was the strongest woman in the world.

"Oh, hell no, fuck you doing lil nigga? Get outta here, this grown folks business! Take yo ass back to yo room cuz you ain't fucking up the vibe in here!"

"Raheem, don't talk to my son like that; he's just a kid and he's scared of the

storm. If he wants to sleep in here, he can. Now, if you can't wait until he goes to sleep, then maybe you're the one that don't need to be here," Rochelle countered.

Raheem chuckled as he eyed Russell. He licked his lips before responding to Rochelle.

"That's cool but just know if I go, so does this," Raheem stated, holding up a small baggie filled with a tan colored power.

Rochelle's eyes widened as she looked at the bag of heroin. Her mouth watered as she thought about what the high would feel like if she was able to take a hit. She wanted that hit; hell, she needed that hit. And if she let Russell sleep in her room tonight, she wouldn't get it. She had no money to get the drug herself, so she needed Raheem to stay.

"Russ, baby, why don't you go in Travis' room until mommy finishes in here? Then, you can sleep with me. Travis will take care of you and won't let anything happen to you."

Russell's little heart was broken. His mother had never turned him away before, and he didn't know why she was doing it now. His little eyes filled with tears and he cuffed his teddy bear under his arm.

"Mommy, please let me sleep in here. I promise I won't bother you. I'll get in the bed and go right to sleep, I promise," Russell replied weakly.

"Boy, shut up with all that damn crying, didn't she tell you no? Get the fuck outta here and do as she said!" Raheem yelled, grabbing Russell's arm and slinging him out the room, closing the door behind him.

Russell was crushed. He sat on the floor in front of his mother's closed bedroom door and cried uncontrollably. He couldn't understand why his mother was letting the man talk to him like that. Travis, who heard Russell crying, walked out of his room and into the hallway, grabbing his little brother and taking him into his room. Russell's seven-year-old mind didn't understand what was going on, however, with Travis being only three years older, he knew exactly what was happening. Seeing how just a week prior he'd caught Raheem and their mother shooting up in the kitchen late one night.

"Travis, I wanna sleep with mommy. It's too loud outside and I'm scared."

"You can't tonight, Russell, but you can sleep in here with me. It's only thunder, it can't hurt you, and if it tries, then I'll beat its ass," Travis whispered, not wanting his mother to hear the cuss words he was using. Russell smiled and climbed into Travis' bed holding his teddy bear tightly. He always felt safe with *his brother because he knew that no matter what, Travis would always protect him.*

Russell jumped up from his dream breathing hard. Sweat poured from his body, soaking through his t-shirt into his sheets. It had been years since he'd had a nightmare about his childhood and he was happy he'd woken up before his dream had gotten worse. Walking into the bathroom, Russell splashed cool water on his face in an effort to calm down. He didn't know what had triggered the dream; however, he prayed that he wouldn't have another. After changing his pajamas and sheets, he got back into the bed and scrolled through IG before going back to sleep.

CHAPTER EIGHT

Manny dressed in all black as he got ready to place his plan into action. There had been no need for any type of discussion. His brother was dead, and in Manny's eyes, both Fatbar and Raphael had something to do with it. They had to pay. There was no way Manny was gonna let this just slide under the rug with no retaliation. After seeing the way his mother cried at Niko's funeral, Manny knew he would have to man up and ride out. To add insult to injury, none of that side of the family was there, not even Rosa, and she and Niko had been close throughout the years. That alone convinced Manny they all had something to do with Niko's murder. The mix of the pain in his heart and the murder on his mind was a horrible combination for anyone involved in his brother's death.

Reaching into his closet, Manny grabbed two black duffle bags, one in which he filled to the top with guns and the other was packed with clothes and money. Manny vowed to himself not to rest until everyone was dealt with, so he made sure to pack up everything he might need in order to put his plan into motion. After placing the bags into the trunk of his car, Manny got into the driver's seat, placed his 45 on his lap, and pulled off, ready for whatever.

The first place he pulled up to was Fatbar's house, making sure to park down the street in order not to be noticed. Manny watched as four armed guards stood strong outside, watching the surrounding area. *I knew this muthafucka would have niggas guarding his shit. One monkey don't stop no show, that nigga still gonna die,* Manny thought. He gripped his gun tightly, ready to blast off at everyone standing in the way of him getting to Fatbar; however, he knew that wouldn't be smart. As hard as it was, Manny knew he had to wait on the right time.

"I'll be back for yo ass Fatbar, just you watch," Manny spoke before pulling off down the street.

———

Several weeks had passed, and it was finally time for Nakia and Raphael to take Aden home. The two couldn't be happier because their family would finally be complete. Raphael had made sure there would be a few guards posted around the home just in case Manny wanted to come back and avenge his brother's death. Raphael knew Manny would not let this go quietly, and the fact that he had not yet tried to retaliate had him feeling a bit uneasy. He knew he would need to find Manny before he found Nakia, and even though he'd put two men on his head, they had yet to find him.

Raphael hated this was going on and only wished Nakia would have told him what was happening before it got out of hand. He couldn't blame her though; with all the secrets he had, he could see why she kept it to herself. All of that was water under the rug now. At this point, Raphael's only concern was keeping his family safe, so he vowed not to leave their side until his men found Manny.

"Mommy, he's so cute. I am gonna be the best big sister ever," Lexi cooed, doting over baby Aden.

"I know you are baby, I can already see that," Nakia laughed.

"Can I hold him?" Rashaud asked.

"Of course, you can, go wash your hands."

Rashaud ran into the bathroom with the biggest smile on his face. Nakia couldn't do anything but laugh as she watched her children. After everything that happened, Nakia could finally say she was happy again. All three of her children were safely back at home. Raphael had several men watching the house so, not only was she happy, she also felt safe. Nakia knew that with Raphael around, no harm would come to her or her children.

Nakia had just handed Aden off to Rashaud and was teaching him how to hold Aden's head up when the doorbell rang.

"I'll get it babe, you stay in here with them," Raphael announced.

Jalyn walked into the living room a few moments later, greeting Nakia with a hug.

"What up, doe, big sis? I'm so happy Aden is home. I thought I was gonna have to fight them doctors if I came up to that hospital one more time, only for them to tell me I couldn't see my nephew."

"Boy, you crazy," Nakia chuckled, knowing her brother was serious. Jalyn had always treated her children like they were his, so for him not to be able to see Aden in the hospital hurt, and Nakia could tell. As tight as his bond was with Rashaud and Lexi, she knew Aden wouldn't be any different.

"Let my hold my nephew," Jalyn said.

"Aww, but Uncle Jay, I just got him," Rashaud wined.

"And you can get him back, after I hold him," Jalyn assured, walking over to him, and picking up Aden. The doorbell rang again, and Raphael went to answer it.

"Dang Aden, everybody wanna come see you today," Nakia spoke, looking over at her precious baby boy.

Raphael returned back to the living room with Rosa right behind him. Rosa was holding several bags in her hand. Nakia smiled and thanked Rosa, knowing the bags were full of items for baby Aden.

"I didn't know what to get him, so I got him every boy item in the baby section," Rosa said, placing the majority of the bags on the floor. "I got you and the kids a little something too," she continued, handing the other three bags to each of them.

"Damn, you ain't get me nothing, sis?" Raphael asked.

"For what? Nakia was the one that had the baby. And kids get gifts because I bought their brother stuff. You know I'm never gonna do for one and not do for the other," Rosa replied.

Raphael couldn't do anything but laugh as he looked down at all the bags. He knew his sister had gone crazy in the stores for her first nephew.

"Y'all should stay for dinner; we were about to order food," Nakia stated.

"I was stayin' for dinner anyway, you already know sis," Jalyn replied.

Rosa nodded her head in agreement before walking over to Jalyn. He smiled at Rosa before placing Aden in her arms. His little body curled up in her arms, as she looked down at him.

"He's so precious," she whispered as she gently ran her hand through his head full of hair. "I love you already," Rosa continued.

The moment warmed Raphael's heart, as he watched the love his sister had for his child grow before his eyes. After everyone agreed on a restaurant, Raphael placed the order. The family sat around the table and enjoyed a great meal as a family.

"I'll wash the dishes," Rosa volunteered.

"And I'll dry," Jalyn announced.

"Thank y'all," Nakia said before standing from the table.

Rosa and Jalyn went to work on clearing the table, as Nakia went to check on Aden. The amount of love in the home gave Nakia a sense of security she hadn't had since the day she and her home were violated.

"You were supposed to call me back last night, what's up with that shit?" Jalyn asked, looking directly into Rosa's eyes. He wasn't used to women blowing him off and wasn't sure how to feel about it. They'd grown close over the last few weeks with them both spending their days and nights at the hospital, and he thought she was feeling him the way he was feeling her.

"Once I got done doing all my shopping, I was so tired that I passed out as soon as I got home," Rosa replied.

Jalyn nodded his head in understanding. After seeing the many bags she'd brought in, he knew she must have been in the stores for hours. Jalyn walked up to Rosa, hugging her from behind. He took in her scent as he pulled her close.

"You should come over to my crib when we leave here. I got something I wanna show you," Jalyn joked.

"Oh yeah? What might that be?" Rosa inquired.

Jalyn pressed his hardness against her plump backside. She smiled and licked her lips as the thoughts of what she could do to his manhood flashed through her mind. She wanted to take him right then and there but opted to wait until they got to his house out of respect for Raphael and Nakia.

"Well, the faster we get these dishes clean, the faster we can go get dirty," Rosa continued.

That was all Jalyn needed. He moved as fast as he could drying and putting away every dish Rosa handed to him. Even though Jalyn and Rosa were only having fun, he liked her and saw her potential. So, he knew that if he let her, she could take his heart. Her cool and laid-back attitude made it easy for him to chill with her; they stayed up for hours on the phone at night talking about anything and everything under the sun. Not to mention, the treasure between her legs was pure gold. He knew he had to be careful if he didn't want to fall for her completely.

"Uncle Jay, you wanna play the game with me?" Rashaud asked, running into the kitchen.

"Not tonight nephew, I got some business to handle. But I can tomorrow, and we can have a long day of just us and the PS5. I'll even bring the snacks," Jalyn proposed.

Rashaud's eyes widened as a huge smile spread across his face. "Will you bring pizza too? Hamburger and onion with parmesan cheese and garlic butter on the crust?" Rashaud asked, calling out his pizza order.

"You already know, nephew, and ranch on the side. I got you."

Rashaud smiled and held out his hand to begin the secret handshake he shared with his uncle. A high five, a low five, two daps and a pound before he exited the kitchen. Rosa couldn't help but smile at Jalyn and Rashaud's interaction. The love he had for his family was beautiful, and Rosa was loving the fact she was witnessing the many layers of his personality.

"Y'all wanna chill out for a minute, maybe have a drink or two. It's a celebration. Nakia and my baby are home!" Raphael cheered.

Both Rosa and Jalyn could see how happy Raphael was and didn't want to let him down. They gave each other a look that said *only for a drink, then we out.*

The three retreated to the living room where Raphael already had the bottle of D'Usse and glasses on the table. Although there were four glasses, Nakia opted out of drinking, letting them know she intended to breastfeed. Raphael nodded before pouring his drink and handing the bottle off to Rosa. They sat around the living room in great conversation until Raphael's phone rang.

"What up, doe?" he answered.

"Yo, it's a car that has circled the street two times already. The second time, it slowed down as it passed the house. It's a dark car, maybe black or blue with dark tint on the windows. That shit don't look right to me, bro, but it's your call on what you want us to do."

"Hold on a minute," Raphael stated, getting up from the couch and walking out the room, not wanting to alert Nakia of any possible danger. The day had been going wonderful, and if it had to end any other way, he didn't want Nakia or the kids to be affected by it.

Once he was in the kitchen and out of Nakia's ear range, he spoke again, "If it come back around again, shoot that muthafucka up. Send two of the men to do a sweep around the neighborhood too and see if the car is still around."

"Say less," the man said before ending the call.

Raphael walked back into the living room, picking up his drink and joining the conversation as if nothing happened.

"You good, bro?" Rosa asked, sensing the uneasy feeling as her brother stepped back into the room.

"Yeah, I'm good sis, it was just a work call," Raphael responded.

Rosa nodded her head and continued to sip her drink. She knew her brother well, so she knew something was up. However, she didn't want to press the issue, so she let it go. Several minutes later, Raphael received a phone call letting him know the car was no longer in the neighborhood. Although Raphael was given the all clear, he knew Manny was the person behind the wheel of the car. Manny had to die; it was unfortunate because he was family, however, it was clear Manny wanted a war that Raphael would be sure to oblige.

———

Nikki stood up from the toilet as she wiped her mouth. This was the third time today that she'd thrown up, and she wondered what she'd eaten to make her feel this way. After brushing her teeth, she went to the kitchen for a sparkling water. Nikki hated throwing up and needed something to settle her stomach. Looking through the fridge to only find still water, she opted to go to the store. There were not a lot of places Cole allowed her to go without him, however, the store was one of the places she could frequent. Thinking the fresh air would do her some good, Nikki put on her shoes and headed out, making sure to leave Cole a note alerting him of her whereabouts, just in case he came home before she'd gotten back.

While walking down the aisles being sure to pick up anything they needed, she passed the pregnancy tests. It wasn't til that moment that she even thought about the fact she just might be pregnant. There had been so much going on that Nikki couldn't even remember the last time she'd even had a period. Picking up a two-pack of the tests, she placed it into her basket, silently praying for the tests to come back negative.

Once Nikki got home, she rushed to the bathroom and immediately sat on the toilet. Hands shaking so rapidly, she could hardly hold the test steady as she waited to see the results. She was praying that only one line would be visible, but just as she was bringing her prayer to a close, the second line popped up. She damn near fell over as she saw it. As if on cue, Cole walked into the apartment slamming the door behind him. Nikki could tell he was upset about something and knew that if she didn't stay clear, her face would be what he took his anger out on.

"How the hell can I bring a baby into this shit?" Nikki whispered as she held the test in her hand. Tears fell as she wished she could hit the redo button on her life.

Not knowing what to do, Nikki rolled the test up into the bathroom tissue and placed it in the bottom of the garbage. She walked out the bathroom just as Cole was about to knock on the door. She jumped as his presence startled her, and she tried to laugh it off.

"Boy, you scared the hell out of me."

"Fuck was you doing in there so long?" Cole questioned as he looked at Nikki skeptically.

"I was using the bathroom. What else would I be doing in here?" Nikki stated as she walked around Cole and went into their bedroom. Lying down on the bed, she turned on the TV and went to Hulu, instantly turning on one of her favorite shows, Scandal. She knew if she showed any emotion, Cole would press the issue and she didn't want that. So, she kept her eyes on the TV, even though Cole was staring daggers at her.

"You bet not be fuckin' lyin' to me," Cole shot back.

"Why would I lie about using the bathroom? What else could I possibly be doing in there Cole? You got me all to yourself, with nowhere to go, just like you wanted me. I can't go anywhere even if I wanted to, the least you can let me do is used the bathroom in peace," Nikki stated, looking directly into Cole's eyes. She didn't want any deception to be detected and knew that looking him in the eye would show him she was telling the truth. She needed time to come up with an exit strategy. She knew it wouldn't be easy with Cole watching her every move; however, it was no way around it. It was no longer just her; Nikki had a life growing inside her that she had to protect, and she would do so by any means.

"Bitch, who the fuck are you talking to? You better learn to have some fuckin' respect for yo man before I have to teach you some. I should fuck you up right now, but I'ma let you breathe," Cole warned as he walked away from the door.

Nikki let out a long breath, thankful she'd just avoided the pressure Cole could have applied. She laid there in bed staring at the tv, yet deep in her own thoughts. Her stomach was still flat as a board, so there was still time for her to get away without him knowing. She tried to think back and figure out how far long she was, but it was pointless. Her days, weeks, and months had all run together. There was so much on her plate and she needed to scrap some off and throw it away. Not only would she have to find a way to get away from Cole, but she would also have to find the means to take care of herself and her child. There was no way Nikki would let Cole inflict the same pain on her child as he was inflicting on her.

"Nikki, Nikki, get yo ass out here!" Cole yelled to her from the living room.

Rolling her eyes yet still getting up from the bed, Nikki walked out into the living room and waited to see what Cole wanted. He looked her up and down as if she knew she was hiding something. Nikki's heart beat through her chest as she waited on Cole to speak. *God, I hope this nigga didn't find that test,* Nikki though to herself, as beads of sweat began to form on her forehead. It was like Cole knew something and was holding out just to see how long it would take her to crack.

"Fix me something to eat, a nigga hungry," Cole stated.

Relief spread across Nikki's face as she went into the kitchen and happily prepared dinner. If that was all he wanted, she would cook for him ten times over; she was just happy her cover wasn't blown. Nikki began to pull pots and pans out of the cabinet before placing the chicken wings in cool water.

"Nah, do it naked," Cole announced.

"Huh?" Nikki asked, looking over at Cole perplexed.

"Take all yo fuckin' clothes off and cook my dinner while I watch you."

The look in Cole's eyes let Nikki know not to test him. She began slowly peeling out of her clothes while Cole's eyes roamed every inch of her body. He took a seat at the table with a glass filled with dark liquor.

"Now, start cookin'," Cole stated once Nikki was fully nude.

Cole had seen her body dozens of times, however, this felt degrading. His dark eyes gawking at her made her feel like dozens of insects were crawling all over her body. She wanted to protest; however, the combination of him drinking and already being mad would send hell fire throughout their home, and Nikki knew it would all land on her. Cole pulled out a small baggie half filled with what Nikki knew to be coke. He poured a small amount on his finger and brought it to his nose, making it disappear within seconds.

"Where did you go today? You thought it was okay to leave this house without me?" Cole asked.

"Huh? Nikki asked, not wanting to look Cole in the eye.

"Bitch, if you can huh, you can hear."

"Oh, um, I just went to the store. I needed a few things and didn't know when you would be back. I left you a note," Nikki replied.

Nikki's hands shook as she tried to clean the chicken wings. She prayed he'd not found the pregnancy tests in the trash before she'd gotten a chance to take it out. She looked over at him trying to read his face, but all she saw was the back of his hand coming down her face. It had all happened so fast that she didn't even see him get up from the table. Nikki instantly fell to the floor, cuffing her cheek in her hand.

"You lyin' ass bitch, so you went to the store and then had to come home and go directly in the bathroom? What you had to do, wash that nigga sex off you?" Cole yelled, pulling Nikki up by her hair and knocking her right back down again. Nikki screamed out in pain as she hit the floor hard.

"Cole, please, stop. I wasn't with nobody, I was at the store," Nikki pleaded.

"You a lyin' ass lil bitch, and you must think I'm stupid. Any other time, you would call me to pick up what you wanted. Now, all of a sudden, yo big bad ass wanna go to the store yoself. And how the fuck you get there?" Cole continued to yell.

Without waiting on a reply, Cole pulled off his belt with one swift motion, wrapping the strap around his hand and allowing the thick buckle to dangle in front of Nikki's face. Her eyes widened, knowing just what Cole was about to do.

"Cole, please, I'm telling you the truth, I really went to the store. I had to use the bathroom really bad when I came back, so that's what I did. I swear I wasn't with anyone else. I wouldn't do that," Nikki beseeched. She wanted him to look into her eyes and see she was telling the truth. She prayed if he would just look into her eyes, he would see that all of this was unnecessary. However, Nikki's pleads fell on deaf ears as Cole lifted his hand, sending the belt buckle rushing across her chest.

"Ahhhh!" Nikki yelled out in pure agony as the buckle collided with her flesh.

"Bitch, you thought you could just play me?" Slap! "You thought you could still be out there fuckin' with them niggas and have me in here payin' all yo fuckin' bills?" Slap! Cole sent the belt buckle down after every sentence, hitting Nikki in a different spot each time. Her skin felt like it was on fire, and all she could do was scream.

"You still fuckin' with that nigga Russell, ain't you? You still out there trickin' for him? Bitch, I should kill you and him for thinkin' y'all can play with me."

Nikki felt all the breath she had left in her body leave at the mention of Russell's name. Out of all the things he could have said, Nikki never thought that Russell's name would be one. The fear shocked her so badly that the next few hits, Nikki didn't even feel. It wasn't until Cole told her he was going to talk to Russell himself.

"Cole, please don't tell him where I am. I swear to you I wasn't with Russell or anyone else. I went to the store for a pregnancy test," Nikki informed.

Those words made Cole stop in his tracks. She could see his dark eyes shine with a spec of light, and that had given her a glimmer of hope. She knew that if she could just get to the pregnancy tests, he would know she was telling the truth.

"I left the test in the bathroom and I was going to surprise you later on tonight."

Nikki knew she had him with those words as she scrambled to her feet and walked to the bathroom, thankful Cole wasn't right behind her. If he would have been, she would have to explain why it was in the trash. Walking back into the kitchen with the test in her hand, she held it up to show Cole her evidence.

"Damn Nic, why wouldn't you just say this shit first? Fuck you let me beat on you like that for? See, you make me like this. It's like you be wantin' me to beat on you or some shit. You should of led with this."

Nikki felt defeated as she watched Cole turn from hard to soft within minutes. Yes, she had played the only card she had to save her life; however, she felt as though she might be putting her baby's life at risk now. This might have stopped him from beating her tonight, however, what would happen the next time he got mad and wanted to take it out on her? Nikki knew this would be the last time he hit her, and she was prepared to stand on that.

CHAPTER NINE

After spending weeks hiding in boats and days at raunchy motels in Italy, Tianna and Tiny had finally made it back to the United States. Although they were in New York and Tianna had no clue how she would get back to Michigan where she had people who could help, a huge weight was lifted from her shoulders. They were walking down the street with nowhere to go when Tiny remembered the sack that Darden handed her right before he'd gotten shot. There was money in it.

"Let's find a bathroom," Tiny said, walking towards a small diner at the corner of the street. The two ladies walked inside and headed right to the back of the restaurant, entering the bathroom and locking the door behind them. Tiny pulled wads of money out the bag and began to count it. Tianna's eyes widened as she looked at all the bills. Relief came over her knowing the money would get them a place to stay and food to eat. She didn't know how much it was, but from the look of the bills, it would be enough to set them up until they figured out their next move.

"This is sixty-thousand Albanian Lek," Tiny announced.

"How much is that in American dollars? Girl, we gotta get that shit switched over, get us some food and a comfortable place to sleep. It was a currency exchange by the port, just about a mile back," Tianna informed. Tiny nodded her head and the pair left the diner, headed back to the port.

"Girl, I can't wait to get this money. I need a hot ass shower and a plush ass bed to sleep in. Shit, between the brothel and the escape, I haven't had a good night's rest in months. Hell, with this kind of money, we can get us a room at one of them fancy ass hotels in Manhattan. We can order some room service and eat it in the complimentary white robes. I think this new found money got my taste buds feeling rich. What you think about lobster and crab legs?" Tianna asked, walking up the street with her head held high as if her feet wasn't just hurting ten minutes ago.

"That shit does sound good, drowned in butter. Mmmm. I need that shit now for real," Tiny stated, rubbing her stomach.

Once they got to the currency exchange, they both walked up to the window. Since Tiny was the only one with a passport, she took the lead and told the clerk why they were there. She handed the older gentleman the money and smiled as the machine counted them out. Once the man had the grand total of the Albanian Lek, he punched in a few keys on his keypad and waited a beat while the computer generated the U.S. dollar amount.

"Okay, looks like this all comes to five-hundred-sixty-two dollars and fifty-three cents," the man stated with a smile.

Both Tianna's and Tiny's mouths dropped simultaneously. Tiny had to rub her ears to assure she was hearing the man correctly. *There's no way all that money only comes to five hundred dollars. Fuck we gonna do with that?*

"I'm sorry sir, I'ma need you to repeat that because it sounds like you said it was only five hundred and sixty-two dollars?" Tianna asked, moving Tiny to the side and standing directly in the window.

"Yes, and here you are," the man said, sliding the money through the slot.

"Fuck we gonna do with five hundred and sixty-two dollars?" Tianna asked, snatching the money from the slot.

Tiny dropped her head in defeat, knowing they wouldn't get far in New York with only five hundred dollars between the two of them.

Just when she thought things were looking up for them, they were knocked right back down. Yes, they had made it back into America, but at what cost? She was pregnant with no money, and the father of her child was dead. At this point, Tiny couldn't even take care of herself. She didn't even have a place to stay, so she had no clue how she would provide for her child.

"Oh, ma'am, my mistake! I apologize, wait one moment!" the man called out, stopping the women before they'd walked away.

They both turned around with a smile on their faces. *Yeah, you damn straight you made a mistake. I knew that money was worth way more than what he gave us. That muthafucka thought he was 'bout to get over on us,* Tianna thought to herself as she walked back up to the window.

"I forgot to give you your fifty-three cents," he announced, placing the change through the slot.

If looks could kill, the man would have been dead twice over at the way Tianna and Tiny stared daggers at him. Tiny wanted to put hands on the man, but the thick glass he was behind saved him. They both stormed off, walking away from the clerk with anger seeping through their pores.

"Well, there goes our fancy hotel in Manhattan with that lobster dinner we wanted," Tiny stated disappointedly.

"We gotta find a motel; we can't stay out here on these streets like this. We been walkin' for hours, and I know you need some rest and some food for that baby," Tianna announced.

Tiny nodded her head in agreement, and the two women walked the streets in an effort to find a cheap motel room. About forty-five minutes into their walked, they stumbled upon a small motel that advertised a weekly stay for two hundred and fifty dollars. The motel looked like a rat trap and reminded Tianna of that series *Bates' Motel.* However, it was the only place they could afford, so they had no choice but to rent the room. After paying for a room, Tianna went to go get food from the small restaurant across the street as Tiny showered.

The sweatpants and t-shirt she wore didn't show any skin at all; however, Tianna noticed the many eyes on her as she walked the short distance to the restaurant. *Damn, if it's one thing niggas gonna do is look for some pussy. They don't care how you dress, a nigga gonna look*, she thought to herself as she laughed silently.

Just then, it was like a lightbulb went off in her head. Tianna knew exactly how to make money because if it was one thing about niggas, they were the same no matter where they came from.

Tiny was out the shower and sitting on the bed flicking through the channels when Tianna walked in holding the bag of food. "You go head and eat. I'ma shower, then I'll eat after."

Walking into the bathroom, Tianna turned on the hot water before taking off her clothes. She got in and let the water run down on her body. This had been the first time in weeks she'd had a hot shower, and she was going to fully enjoy every minute, not getting out until the water turned cold.

Tianna grabbed her food, sat on her bed and started eating. She felt so much better after the hot shower and knew that after a good night's rest, she would be rejuvenated.

"How much money do we got left?" Tianna asked, looking over at Tiny.

"Shit, not that much. Bout two-fifty, if that," Tiny answered. "What we gonna do, girl? That's not even enough for another week here, and we still gonna have to eat every day. This shit is fucked up. I'm over here pregnant with a dead baby daddy and no way to take care of me or my child. What the fuck are we gonna do? We should have just stayed at the damn brothel. At least then we would have a warm place to sleep and a hot meal every day."

Tianna could see the tears forming in Tiny's eyes and knew she was scared. Hell, so was she but at least she didn't have a child that she would have to take care of.

"Nah, fuck that, we had to get out of that damn place. That shit would have killed us if we didn't. I know it don't seem like it right now, but we gonna be okay. Tiny, do you trust me?" Tianna asked.

"Huh, what you mean?" Tiny asked, perplexed.

"What if I told you I knew a way we could get a lot of money and fast?"

"Well, bitch, start talkin' because the little money we got ain't gonna get us nowhere," Tiny replied, turning to face Tianna, and giving her undivided attention.

"See, that's the thing; we gonna need that money so that we can make some more money. Just hear me out. I can already see you not being with it by the look on your face," Tianna said, noticing the skeptical look Tiny was giving her.

"If we use the money we got to get a phone, we can start our own business just like I did before I got sent to Albania. I was makin' over five thousand a week, and that was just workin' four days a week. I'm tellin' you, Tiny, if it's one thing I know, it's how to make some money off these niggas. Because I know for a fact that pussy runs everything. Just fuck with me, Tiny. I promise you we not gonna even need another week in this motel. We gonna have enough money to get us an Airbnb to work out of, just like I had back home, but we gotta start now. And it ain't no half steppin'. We gotta work like our lives depend on it because they do. Just trust me, Tiny."

Tiny looked at Tianna in deep thought as she processed everything Tianna had just told her. She wanted to believe her plan could work, but at the same time, she was scared to put up all the money they had for it. It was only a fifty/fifty chance that it would work; there was no guarantee. However, there was a guarantee that if they didn't make any money, they would be broke once it ran out. Tiny knew that it took money to make money, so with that, she agreed to Tianna's plan. They both decided they would find a Metro PCS store and get the cheapest phone they had first thing the next morning.

Russell watched as Deja strolled in the double door at the Saint Regis hotel. Since she'd came on his team, Deja and her crew had pulled in almost six figures, which was more than he was used to making with any other girl he had. Deja was on top of her game and had completely leveled Russell up in the short time they'd been working together. He still had Hannah around, but the money she brought in was chump change compared to what he was getting now. He had started spending all his time making sure Deja and her crew was good, so he'd completely put Hannah on the back burner. She was setting up her own jobs and going to them by herself. If it wasn't for the money she slid under his door every night, he wouldn't have even known she was still there.

Russell had just gotten into a parking space as he saw a familiar car pull into the parking lot. *What is this nigga doing here, is his ass following me?* Russell thought to himself as he watched Travis' car pull in. Russell watched him get out, walk around to the passenger side, and open the door. A slim-thick light-skinned woman got out. Russell had never seen her before, however, something about her looked very familiar. The two walked arm in arm through the doors and didn't even see Russell watching their every move.

"I don't know what type of shit you on bro, but I'm definitely gonna figure that shit out," Russell spoke out loud, feeling as though his brother was somehow working against him. Russell's phone rang, breaking him from the deep thought he was in.

"What up, doe?" he answered.

"R-Russell, I need you to come get me," Hannah whispered into the phone.

"Hannah? Is that you? Fuck you whispering for? I can barely hear you."

"Russell, I need you to come get me. The John I went to go see has three more men in here with him. Russell, I'm scared. I locked myself in the bathroom and they keep saying if I don't come out, they will break down the door and pull me out. I tried to give the guy his money back and just leave when I found out it was more than one, but they wouldn't let me go. He's telling me I have to service all four of them or they're going to rape me. Please Russell, I'm so scared."

"Wait, Hannah, slow down. Are you at a hotel or a house? I'm going to need your location in order to come get you," Russell stated.

"Bitch, you got ten seconds to come out that fuckin' bathroom before we come the fuck in there!"

Russell could hear the men yelling at her from outside the door.

"Yes, I'm at a hotel. Russell, please come get me, I don't know what else to do. I just sent you the address and room number. I'm so fucking scared," Hannah cried.

Russell could hear the fear in her tone and told her he would be there in ten minutes, making her promise to stay in the bathroom until he got there. He rushed out of the parking lot speeding down the street in an effort to get to Hannah as fast as he could. He knew that anything could happen in the time it took him to get there, and he just prayed it wouldn't be anything bad. He had been in such a rush to get to Hannah that he didn't even text Deja and let her know he left. *Damn, I hope she's not done before I get back,* he thought to himself.

Exactly ten minutes later, Russell was pulling up to the old motel where Hannah was. Pulling his pistol out of his middle console, Russell quickly got out his car and ran up to the door of room 6. His heart dropped when he saw the door was slightly ajar. He used the butt of his gun to open the door all the way before stepping in. The entire room looked like a tornado had run through it. Lamps were broken on the floor, the television was across the room, and the bed had no linen on it whatsoever.

"Hannah!" Russell called out as he slowly walked through the room. When she didn't answer, he called her name a little louder. It wasn't until Russell almost tripped and fell that he found her. There lying on the floor alongside the bed was a lifeless Hannah.

"No, no, no, please, God no! Hannah, please get up," Russell spoke, shaking her.

When she didn't respond, Russell already knew what was up. Hannah was dead. There was nothing he could do to help her because she was already gone. As much as he didn't want to, he knew with him being on papers, he couldn't be anywhere near this crime scene. Although he hated leaving her like that, there wasn't anything else he could do. With that, Russell walked out the door, got in his car and headed back to the Saint Regis.

It had been years since Russell had shed tears but that night when he got in his room alone, that's exactly what he did. He cried for Hannah, knowing she would never have a proper send off. With her not having any family, she would definitely go in the books as a Jane Doe, then buried in the cemetery of the lost and never found. She had spent her life by Russell's side, and he felt like pure shit for not being

74

by her side at least in death. Russell cried himself to sleep that night, curled up in his bed like a small child.

———

"Mama, I'm home from school. Travis stayed after, so he could try out for the basketball team," Russell announced cheerfully as he swung his backpack on the couch.

"What you cooking for dinner mama? It smells good and I'm hungry," Russell continued.

"Yo mama not here. She told me that you and I need to spend some time together and get to know each other better," Raheem said, walking into the living.

Russell looked up at Raheem skeptically, as if he knew he was lying. His mother had never left him home alone with anyone, and the fact it was Raheem didn't sit right with him. Even as a child, he was able to read the energy people put out, and this time was no different. Something wasn't right, and Russell could feel it.

"Ma!" Russell yelled as he began walking through the house. When he got to his mother's room door, he opened it and saw his mother lying in her bed.

"Mama, why you in bed and why Raheem tell me you wasn't home?" Russell asked, jumping up onto the bed next to his mother.

"Because, you need to spend some time with Raheem. He likes you and want to get to know you better. Raheem might be around for a long time, so it's only right for you and your brother to form a bond with him," Rochelle explained.

"But I don't like him, and I don't want to get to know him. He looks like a bad man, mama."

Rochelle sat up and looked at her son. She knew that what she was about to do would deem her a horrible and unfit mother, but to her, she saw no other way. In her mind, Raheem was paying her bills and feeding her now sixty dollar a day drug addiction. He'd never asked her for anything in return, so when he did ask for something, Rochelle had no choice but to oblige, even if what he was asking for was her seven-year-old son.

"Russell, do you love mommy?" she asked.

"You know I love you, mommy. You my bestest mommy in the whole wide world," Russell replied, unknowingly feeding right into Rochelle's manipulation.

"Would you do anything for mommy?"

"Yes, mommy, I would do any and everything in the world for you. I love you, mommy."

"Then, do what Raheem wants you to do. If you do that, then it would help mommy out a lot. Mommy is real sick. That's why I'm in bed. But if you go out there and do what Raheem says, then he will give me the medicine I need, and I won't be sick anymore," Rochelle stated.

Russell looked up at her and frowned, not understanding why Raheem wouldn't just give her the medicine she needed.

"You can save the day and be the superhero I always knew you was," Rochelle continued.

"I can be a superhero? Like, a real life one mommy?" Russell cheered as his little eyes widened.

"Yes, baby, a real-life superhero."

"Okay mama, I'ma go do everything he say and get you your medicine. I'll come back in here later and make sure he gave it to you. I'm about to go save the day!" Russell cheered as he left the room, not knowing his innocence would be left there as well.

CHAPTER TEN

The light shined in from the window, waking Nakia from a sound sleep. Rolling over and looking at her clock, she saw it was nine in the morning. She couldn't believe no one else in the house was awake yet. She smiled at Raphael as she looked over at him sleeping so peacefully and decided to cook a big breakfast for her family. Grabbing her phone, she went down to the kitchen and connected her phone to the small Bluetooth speaker she kept there. She turned on her music and began cooking.

Nakia's phone rang, disturbing her vibe. She quickly answered it, trying to get back to the Beyoncé song that had been playing.

"Hello?" Nakia said, placing the phone to her ear.

"Nakia, I have been trying to get in touch with you for several weeks. I was about to do a welfare check and come to your house."

"Excuse me? Who the hell is this?" Nakia asked confused.

"This is Special Agent Scott. The trial is just two weeks away. As an individual who has been subpoenaed to testify, I have to inform you that if you don't testify, there will be a warrant issued for you for obstruction of justice. Once that happens, I can guarantee that you will be arrested," Agent Scott informed.

Nakia looked down at her phone and rolled her eyes. She was sick of this agent trying to strong arm her into testifying. It was as if he needed Nakia to do his job for him without her getting the pay and protection he had. She'd almost lost her life and all he could do was threaten jail time on her. She was at her wits end and could care less about the FBI needing her help.

"Listen, Agent Scott, you have already given me the subpoena. It has the date, time, and location of the trial, so there is no need for you to keep calling me multiple times a day. This is beginning to become harassment and I don't take too kindly to that. Please refrain from calling me anymore until the day of trial, thank you," she replied before ending the call and turning back on her music.

Nakia had already made a pact with Bailey not to testify, so without the two of them, the prosecution would have to put in work in order to convict Russell. That sounded like a "them" problem to her, so she continued to snap her fingers and cook to Beyoncé.

"What you got goin' on, smelling so good down here?" Raphael asked, walking into the kitchen. He hugged and kissed Nakia lovingly before having a seat at the kitchen island.

"What you doing up? I wanted to have breakfast done before y'all woke up. Are the kids up?"

"I just fed Aden and he went back to sleep; Rashaud and Lexi still knocked out," Raphael replied.

"Okay good. Babe, I've been thinking. What do you think about us getting a house in Mexico?"

"Mexico? Why Mexico? I didn't know you wanted to move outside the country," Raphael asked, clearly confused.

"I just think it would be nice for us to have a house out of the country. We can go now while the kids are out of school for the summer. I'm not saying sell this house, but with everything that went on in here, I need a break from my surroundings. I'm just saying we should get another house as more of a vacation home if you will," Nakia stated.

"Is that what you really want? Will that make you happy?" Raphael asked, looking her in the eyes.

Nakia nodded and he understood that Nakia may need a change of scenery after almost losing her life in that very house. So, he would do any and everything he could in order to give her exactly what she needed.

"Then, that's what we're going to do. I got some runs to make today, but when I get back, we can get online and start looking for places," Raphael informed.

Nakia smiled, walking over to Raphael hugging him tightly. She was so happy that this man was hers and knew he would do anything to make her happy. He didn't have to know the real reason she wanted to go was because she didn't want to testify in a trial.

Once everyone had eaten and the dishes were washed, Raphael went up to get dressed for his day. He needed to go see Fatbar and get information on Russell. Raphael knew he was the reason any of this was happening and wanted to pay him a visit and have a little chat. Raphael kicked himself repeatedly for not knowing what was going on in his own home, and he vowed that would never happen again. There had been too many secrets, and Raphael knew it was coming down to the time they would all be in the open, and he would start with his own. However, first, he had to assure that his family would be safe. He knew Manny had been driving past his house and knew he had some shit up his sleeve as well. Raphael knew he would see him as well, and when he did, whatever Manny wanted to happen could. Just as long as he kept his family out of it.

Raphael pulled up to his childhood home and waved to the guards outside before pulling into the driveway. His mother greeted him at the door, purse in hand.

"Where you on yo way to, mama?" Raphael asked, greeting his mother with a hug.

"Just out to do a little shopping. It's been too much going on here; I need to get away," Harlin replied.

"Make sure you take a guard with you. You're not going out alone," Fatbar countered, walking up to the door after Harlin.

Harlin rolled her eyes before she replied, "Fatbar, I'm a grown woman, and I can take care of myself. I'm going out today to get away from all this, and you want me to take it with me? Not gonna happen. I'll be fine. Nobody is looking for me anyway," Harlin spoke out in irritation.

"Them lookin' for us is them looking for you. You know that, mama. Pops is right; you need to take a guard with you, hell, maybe even two," Raphael stated.

Harlin let out a loud breath, wishing Fatbar and Raphael would just let her be. However, she knew there was no way they would let her out the house without guards with her. So, instead of continuing to protest, she agreed, hugging both her husband and her son before walking to the car.

"So, what's up son? What brings you here today?"

"Does mama know everything that's going on? Cuz she movin' like she don't," Raphael stated.

"She knows that Niko is dead but don't know he was found in your home. She also doesn't know that Manny's on our heads or that Nakia was a witness in Russell's case," Fatbar answered.

"Oh, then she don't know anything. You need to tell her, Pops, so she's in the loop. And while we talkin' 'bout Russell, I need you to set up a meeting with him and me. This nigga brought a lot of trouble to my household and family. Because of him, the family is beefin' and Nakia is walkin' around scared for her life. On top of that, he sent my own cousin to kill my bitch and our child. Yeah, I'ma need to see him," Raphael said.

"Yeah, I knew you wasn't just coming over here to see how your father was doing," Fatbar joked. "Look Raphael, I get why you wanna holla at Russell. Hell, I would too if I was you. However, I think you should focus on one problem at a time, and right now, our biggest problem is Manny. That man is family and been on our team for years. Which means he knows how we move, he knows how we fight. That muthafucker probably knows that we standing here right now talking about his ass. Son, I'm not saying don't get at Russell because I agree that you need to. I'm just saying we need to get Manny before he gets us, and then we can get at Russell," Fatbar suggested.

Raphael nodded his head, knowing his father was right. Manny was clearly the bigger threat. Russell was no murderer; Raphael knew that because he and Niko had been sent to do that job for him. However, Manny, on the other hand, had a murder game so strong, he would put any serial killer to shame. Raphael knew Manny was putting together a plan at that very moment to take them all out, so he needed to get at him first.

"You right Pops, but how we gonna find him? I know that nigga ain't just sittin' at home waiting on us. Yeah, he might know how we move, but don't forget; we know how he moves as well. I taught that man everything he knows. So, I know he not at home waiting on us to get at him. He out there somewhere staked out waitin' to get at us."

"Exactly, and that's what we have to let him do. Let him come to us so that we can take him out. Trust me when I tell you he will be at one of our doorsteps very soon, and when he does, that will be our chance to go in for the kill," Fatbar spoke.

Raphael nodded his head, knowing that was probably their best plan seeing how they had no idea of Manny's whereabouts. He would definitely come to them though, and when he did, they would all be ready.

———

Harlin pulled her car into the cemetery and parked. It hurt her deeply that she couldn't be at her nephew's funeral, and she didn't understand why. Fatbar had told her things were too dangerous and to not question him, so she didn't, although it hurt her to do so. Harlin knew her husband wouldn't have made her miss it if he didn't really think danger was lurking. However, the fact that he'd yet to tell her what the danger was had Harlin on edge. She hated lying to her husband, but there was no other way for her to get out the house and pay her respects to her nephew. Grabbing the flowers she'd purchased, she got out of her car and began walking towards the grave.

"Ms. Harlin, I have strict orders for us not to be here. This is a very dangerous situation, and I think we should leave now," Blue stated, getting out the car and standing next to Harlin.

"I appreciate your concern Blue; however, I am a grown woman. My nephew is resting here. I didn't go to the funeral due to whatever my husband has going on. I'll be damned if anyone tells me I can't pay my respects to my nephew today on his birthday. I've always spent time with him every year on his birthday since the day he was born, and today won't be any different. Now, you can either come with me or stay in the car," Harlin spoke, walking away.

Manny watched from his car, as Harlin walked up to Niko's grave. He was just about to go put flowers on his brother's resting place when he saw none other than his auntie pull up. He could see there was another person with her and he hoped like hell it was Fatbar or Raphael. His trigger finger itched as he waited for the passenger to step into his line of sight. Manny shook his head when he realized it was only Blue, a shooter from his Uncle's payroll. Placing his pistol back on his lap, he watched as the two of them talked before Harlin walked away. He knew at that moment, he had the upper hand. He could take her life right now, and both Fatbar and Russell would be devastated. However, it wasn't enough for them to know their loved one was dead; Manny needed them to see it happen.

Harlin placed the flowers down on the ground as tears fell from her eyes. The fact Niko was no longer here was breaking her, and she had no clue how or when she would become whole again. Losing Niko was like losing one of her own children. When Niko was a baby, he spent so much time with Harlin, everyone thought he was her child. Now, she would never get another minute with him again.

"Fatbar is going to tell me what happened to you tonight. I'm not keeping my mouth closed anymore," Harlin whispered.

"Harlin spent the rest of the afternoon sitting and talking with her nephew, not knowing her other nephew was lurking in the shadows plotting to take out the entire family. Before leaving, Harlin kissed Niko's headstone and walked to her car.

CHAPTER ELEVEN

Russell hadn't been the same since Hannah was murdered. He missed the shit out of her and was sad that he didn't treat her the way he should have while she was alive. He knew he was at fault for what happened to her. She never wanted to go to see the Johns without him, however, when he started getting money with Deja, it was as though Hannah didn't exist to him. He was making so much money with Deja and her girls that he really could have let Hannah go her own way. Instead, he kept her around, and now, she was dead.

"What up, doe bro, you up?" Travis asked, knocking on Russell's door in a pattern before entering the room. "Damn, you okay bro? You look like you just lost yo best friend."

Russell looked over at him, tears in his eyes that he tried not to let fall down his cheeks. He felt so guilty and couldn't shake the feeling no matter how hard he tried. In a way, he had indeed lost his best friend. Hannah had been down with him since day one and stayed that way no matter what. There weren't a lot of people in the world like that, and Russell had taken the one he was blessed with for granted. As hard as it was to do, Hannah had truly loved Russell. Once he realized it, it was too late, and Russell knew he would never have love like that again.

"Hannah's dead," Russell replied.

"What? How? When? I just saw her the other day. Man, what the fuck happened Russell? Fuck you do to that lil girl?" Travis asked, not believing what was being told to him.

"Fuck you just say? Fuck you mean what did I do to her?" Russell walked up to Travis, looking him directly in the eyes while waiting on him to answer.

"Bro, we both know how you are with yo girls. You literally had me with you while you tried to chase two of them down, just so they wouldn't stop hoeing for you. I just asked you what happened to her," Travis stated, holding his hands up in surrender.

"I would have never hurt Hannah! She was the definition of a down ass bitch. She was killed by a john. She called me scared about the john she'd went to see. I was with Deja at the time, but I left soon as she called. Maaan, by the time I got there, she was already gone."

Repeating the words out loud, Russell couldn't help but to break down. Saying it out loud made it so real, and Russell could no longer hold it in. The tears he was trying so hard not to let fall from his eyes were now flowing like rivers. Travis, who hadn't seen his brother this way in years, couldn't help but to hug him. He could tell his brother was hurting and he hated that for him.

"Damn Russ, I'm sorry this shit happened. I know you blamin' yourself right now, but you can't do that. It was just her time. If it hadn't happened this way, it would have been another. You gotta remember bro, God don't make no mistakes. Chin up. You gonna be good."

"Thank you, bro. I needed that," Russell responded.

"I was comin' up here to see if you wanted to go get some drinks. I had no idea all this shit was going on. I wanted you to meet my girl since you the only family I got. But that shit can wait if you not feelin' up to it. We can just go grab a few drinks together if you want to," Travis suggested.

"I'll do anything to try to take my mind off this shit. And bring yo girl, I'd love to meet her. Maybe I'll bring someone, too. We can make it a double date so I'm not the third wheel," Russell joked.

"Cool, I'ma go get dressed and pick her up, call me when you ready and we can meet somewhere," Travis stated before leaving the room.

———

Deja pulled into the parking lot of the lofts where Remy resided and got out the car. The long pink sundress she wore swayed with her hips as she walked. Deja was beautiful and captured everyone's attention as she walked by without even trying. She'd just walked inside Remy's home when her cell phone rang.

"Hello?" Deja answered.

"What up, doe, it's Russell. What you doin' tonight? You busy?"

"Hey Russell, I'm just chillin' tonight. I just got to Remy's house, bout to chill with her for a few. Why, what's up?"

"My brother wants to introduce me to his new girlfriend over drinks and I don't want to be the third wheel. I wanted to know if you was down to go with me," Russell asked.

"Umm, yeah, we can do that. I need to get dressed first. What time you thinkin'?"

"Yeah, I gotta get dressed too, so maybe about a couple hours from now. Let's say about nine-ish. I'll hit you up when I'm dressed and I'll come pick you up. Cool?"

"Yeah, that sounds good to me. I'll see you later," Deja replied before ending the call.

"Where he want you to go, now?" Remy asked, overhearing Deja's side of the conversation.

"Out for drinks with his brother and his brother's girlfriend."

"Oh yeah? You mean like a double date? That nigga likin' on you. Don't mix business with pleasure now Deja, that never comes out good. We all have a job to do here," Remy stated seriously.

"I'm all about doin' the job Rem. In order to do that job, I have a role to play. Me goin' out for drinks with him and his brother is me playin' my role," Deja answered.

Remy nodded her head in agreement, knowing Deja was right. They'd put this plan into motion together and they all had to make sure they executed it accordingly. One false move and everything they had worked so hard for could crumble, and that was what Remy didn't want. However, she knew how skilled Deja was, so she was just going to have to trust her.

———

A few hours later, Russell was picking Deja up from her home. They headed to the restaurant where Travis and his girlfriend were already waiting. When they walked in, Russell immediately spotted his brother sitting at the table conversing with a beautiful woman. Russell and Deja walked over to the table and greeted the happy couple.

"Russell, I'm glad y'all was able to join us. This is my girl, Arion. Arion, this is my brother Russell and his friend Deja," Travis introduced.

"Hello, it's nice to meet you both," Arion spoke, extending her hand to shake theirs.

"Hi, it's nice to meet you as well," Deja replied before taking her seat.

The four of them spoke over drinks and good food. They shared laugh after laugh, and Russell was happy that he was finally able to take his mind off of Hannah, even if it was just for a few hours. He could tell his brother was very happy with his new girlfriend and he loved that for him. In that moment, it didn't matter the times they butted heads or didn't see eye to eye. Seeing his brother happy made him happy, and even though Travis didn't know it, he had once again saved Russell from the depression he was just about to slip in just a few hours earlier. Just like when they were kids, Travis had saved Russell, protecting him from things to come.

"I gotta use the ladies' room, I'll be right back," Deja said, standing from the table.

"Oh, well, hold on, I'ma go with you," Arion said, and the two of them walked off.

"I really like her, bro. I almost might love her," Travis stated as he watched Arion walk away.

"Yeah, I can tell. I ain't never heard you give nobody a title before. I thought we was keepin' it pimpin' til the grave and yo ass done went and got cuff'd up," Russell joked.

Travis joined in on Russell's laughter before taking a gulp of his drink and getting serious. "Look bro, I know shit been kinda fucked up between us lately, but you my blood and I ain't gonna let shit come between us."

"Say less, bro. All that shit over, straight like that. We both here right now and that's all that matters."

The two brothers raised their glasses and took a drink, drawing a truce with each other and putting all their differences behind them.

"Do you think we have enough evidence to convict, now? I mean, me, Remy and Sophie been workin' with this nigga for weeks now and you been datin' his brother. I know you been getting' info from his ass. How much longer do you think this is gonna take? His trial is in a couple weeks," Deja whispered as she looked around to make sure no one else was inside the bathroom.

"I've been tryin'. Travis hasn't been sayin' much about him. He hasn't told me more than we already know. I do know ever since he started workin' with y'all, he hasn't fucked with any underage girls. The one girl he did have turned eighteen recently," Arion replied.

Deja, Arion, Sophie and Remy were an all-female task force who specialized in making sure men like Russell spent the rest of their lives in prison. Sex trafficking was bad in itself, but to do it with children was horrible. Deja wanted nothing more than to see Russell rot in prison. Seeing how she had a sister that was involved in sex trafficking, to her, this was personal. Her older sister was kidnapped and sold into that lifestyle at the young age of twelve years old and was found murdered two years later. Deja was only ten at the time and couldn't do much when it came to justice for her own sister. However, at the age of twenty-six, she'd devoted her life to assuring she saved the life of every child she could.

"He was trafficking her while she was underage though, right? It can still stick. Isn't she one of the girls he was caught with anyway?" Deja asked.

"Yeah, that's her."

"Maybe I can get Russell to introduce us, she might be willing to talk," Deja suggested.

"Ummm, I don't know about that Deja. If she tells him you questioning her, that could blow our cover," Arion replied.

"I got this, I just got to meet her. I got the rest. You know damn well I'm not gonna blow our cover after puttin' in all this work. This muthafucka is goin' down, and we gonna make sure of that shit," Deja stated.

"Period pooh," Arion responded, as they laughed and high fived each other.

———

Harlin walked inside her home and saw Fatbar sitting on the couch watching a movie. Her emotions were through the roof, and although she'd been quiet over the past weeks, all that was over. It was time for Fatbar to tell her the truth about what was going on. Placing her purse and keys on the table, she went and took a seat next to him.

"Did you break the bank shopping today?" Fatbar joked, knowing just how expensive his wife's taste could be.

"Fatbar, we need to talk," Harlin spoke in a no-nonsense tone.

"What's on yo mind, baby?"

"Fatbar, I need to know what is going on. My favorite nephew passed and I wasn't allowed to go to his funeral. There our guards outside our home twenty-four hours out of the day. Rosa even told me there's guards outside her house, as well as Raphael's. Fatbar, I'm telling you now, if you had anything to do with Niko being dead, I swear I'll never forgive you," Harlin stated.

Fatbar looked at Harlin and saw the tears in her eyes. He knew she was hurting and he never meant for that to happen. He would do anything to keep Harlin happy, and to know she hurt at the moment bothered him.

"Baby, I promise you I didn't kill Niko. He was my nephew, too, and I loved him just as much as you did. You gotta believe that."

"Then, what the fuck is going on Fatbar? Why the fuck was it too dangerous for me to attend the funeral? Why can't I leave my fucking house without some armed guard tagging along? You gonna have to tell me something, Fatbar."

"All of that is to keep you safe, Harlin. I would fucking die if anything happened to you," Fatbar replied.

"Keep me safe from what? Stop talking in circles Fatbar and tell me what the hell is going on."

Fatbar blew out a long breath and rubbed his hand down his face. He wanted to tell Harlin everything, but he figured the less she knew, the better.

"Baby, I just want to protect you. If you don't know what's going on, then your hands are clean," he countered.

"Listen to me right now Fatbar; I don't give a fuck about none of that shit! What the fuck is going on?" Harlin yelled as she stood to her feet. She was getting tired of repeating herself and was ready to just leave.

Fatbar, knowing he had no other choice, opened his mouth to speak.

"Nakia killed Niko. He was the man that broke into her house the night she went into labor."

"What are you talking about, Fatbar? Why would Niko break into Raphael and Nakia's house?" Harlin asked, perplexed.

"Nakia is a witness in Russell's case. I didn't know it at the time, but I sent Niko and Raphael to kill the witnesses before they could testify against him. Hours had gone past, and I couldn't get in touch with Niko. Then, Raphael called and told me what happened to Nakia. He told me that the man who broke in was still dead in the home at the hands of Nakia. Not knowing where the hell Niko was, I sent Manny to dispose of the body. I had no clue the man would be Niko until Manny called me at the hospital flipping the fuck out."

Harlin's eyes widened as she took in all the information that Fatbar was dishing out.

"Is that what sent you into that heart attack?" Harlin asked.

"Yes, and on top of that, Manny is on our asses. He's not letting that shit go without a fight. I knew if you went to the funeral, it would be like serving you on a silver platter, and I couldn't let that happen. I don't know when he's coming, but I know he is so I gotta stay ready," Fatbar answered.

"Does Rosa and Raphael know this?"

"Raphael does, but I'm not sure about Rosa. As the head of this family, my job is to protect y'all, so that's what I'm doing. I'm not gonna let any harm come to any of you," Fatbar replied.

"You need to let Rosa know. You can't protect her if she doesn't know what the danger is."

"You right, baby. We need to call a family meeting," Fatbar said as he kissed Harlin on the forehead. He had to admit he felt as though a huge weight had been lifted from him. He hated keeping secrets from his wife and had only done so because he thought it was in her best interest. Fatbar and Harlin spent the rest of their night cuddled up on the couch watching movies.

Tianna and Tiny walked back into their motel room with a Metro PCS bag in hand. Tianna was excited because she knew all the money the small cell phone would bring them. She knew this was their way out of the poverty she'd found herself in. Tianna was a pro at this and knew her and Tiny would be up in just a number of days. Since Tiny still wasn't showing at all, she told Tianna that she would work until her stomach got too big.

Tianna wasted no time setting up the website. The two girls got dressed in one of the few skimpy outfits they were able to bring with them and began taking pictures of each other. Once the pictures were uploaded, they sat and waited for their first hit. Within twenty minutes, the phone was vibrating and Tianna was setting up the first appointment. It was a white man that looked to be in his mid to late thirties. He was well dressed in his black tailored suit, and the ring that adorned his left ring finger let Tianna know he was a married man.

Tianna knew the game of the married men and the vanilla sex they had with their wives. They paid women like her to fulfill their sexual fantasies and fetishes, and as long as the money was coming to her, Tianna was more than okay with that.

"Hello, I'm Charles," the john introduced. He eyed Tianna seductively as he licked his lips, becoming immediately turned on by her.

"Hello Charles, it's nice to meet you. I'm whoever you want me to be. Tell me, what did you come here for tonight?" Tianna asked, walking closer to him, and placing her hand on the crotch of his pants. She felt his manhood stiffen as she massaged it in a circular motion.

Charles told Tianna everything he wanted before handing her five hundred dollars. Tiny was supposed to stay in the bathroom until Charles left; however, she'd come out to retrieve a bottled water. Charles' eyes widened when he saw Tiny, as the fantasy of a threesome played in his mind.

"How much for the both of you?" Charles questioned with a raised eyebrow.

Tiny looked over at Tianna and smiled, knowing they'd just stumbled across a serious lick.

"A thousand," Tianna replied.

Without another word, Charles peeled off five more hundred from his wad and handed them to Tianna. Just like that, they'd made a thousand in the first hour of them starting the website, and Tianna knew it was only up from there. By the end of the night, they had racked in more than enough money to get an Airbnb, however, decided to stay in the room for the entire week because the desk clerk refused to give them a refund for the unused nights. That didn't matter to them, though.

They'd come up with a new strategy that seemed to be very lucrative. By promoting their eight-hundred-dollar threesome deal, the man would get two women at a discounted price. Once the men walked in and saw two girls, they wanted them both anyway, so why not allow them to get a discount? That way, they would come back more frequently.

By the end of the week, they had made close to twenty thousand

and were moving into their new four-bedroom Airbnb. Tianna was proud of her and Tiny. They had managed to do for themselves. Russell had thought he could take everything away from her by selling her to the Albanians. Now, she was back in the U.S. making her way back on top. They decided they would take the day off and spend the first night at their Airbnb enjoying their hard work.

CHAPTER TWELVE

Nikki laid in bed staring at the TV, even though she was deep in thought. Her eyes watered as tears fell into the huge bags underneath them. Her sleep had been evaded, and even though it had been a few days since Cole had last beaten her, she was still sore. Yet and still, it wasn't the physical pain that she couldn't handle. The mental pain she was suffering from was too excruciating for her to bear. She felt lower than the fish in the bottom of the ocean and would give anything to have a regular life, one free of manipulation and abuse. However, at this point, Nikki feared that was a life she would never experience. She could only thank God that she'd not suffered a miscarriage from the forceful blows she'd received by Cole's hands. At least once her baby was here, she would have someone to love her, seeing how nobody else around her ever did.

Nikki knew at that moment her baby was a fighter from the fact he or she was able to withstand one of Cole's beatings. However, she promised herself this wouldn't be her child's fight. She rubbed her stomach and whispered to her baby, "Mommy is coming up with a plan to get us out of here. I promise."

Cole had been cool the last couple of days, not even so much as raising his voice to her; however, Nikki was more than fed up. She knew she couldn't go on living like this and would have to do something quickly.

"You want something from the store?" Cole asked, entering their bedroom.

"Nah, I'm good."

"Well, I'ma be gone for a few hours. I want dinner made by the time I get back. Steak and lobster with potatoes and creamed spinach. And make sure you make that butter sauce I like on my lobster," Cole ordered. Nikki nodded her head okay but said nothing. Her mind was still on getting away from Cole.

"Wash the clothes in the hampers. All of them are about full and I'm sick of seein' them," Cole chastised.

"I let you be lazy for a couple days to get yo shit together, but that's over now. It's time for yo ass to do some fuckin' housework," he continued.

Cole didn't give a damn how Nikki felt. In his eyes, she had a job to do, and that was to take care of him. Whether she liked it or not, that was exactly what she was going to do.

Nikki didn't say a word, just continued to stare at the TV. Cole knew she had heard him, though, so he didn't repeat himself. Nikki knew what would happen if she didn't do everything he'd said, so he just walked away, leaving the house to start his day.

"It's not gonna be too much longer that I put up with this shit," Nikki spoke, getting up from bed and taking the lobster tails and steaks from the freezer and putting them in cool water to unthaw.

Heading to the closet, Nikki began separating the clothes and going through the pockets of all the pants. She wanted to hurry up and get the laundry and food done, so she could lie back in bed. Reaching her hands into the pockets of a pair of Cole's jeans, Nikki pulled out a small baggie with six tiny blue pills inside. Nikki had been around the block enough to know Fentanyl when she saw it. Nikki smiled as she held the baggie up in front of her face and shook it. Nikki suddenly became happy as she put together a plan in her head.

After all the clothes were washed and put away, Nikki started on dinner. She seared the steaks before seasoning the lobster and placing them inside the broiler. Nikki even turned on the radio and blasted music throughout the home as she cooked and cleaned, dancing around to the beat in a little two step she put together. Once the table was set, it was time for Nikki to prepare the butter sauce Cole requested. Grabbing a larger can of baked beans from her panty, Nikki put the baggie of pills on the counter and used the can to crush them up. It took her about five minutes to crush all the pills into powder form, and once she did, she stirred it into the sauce. Nikki smiled, knowing she'd just came across her way out.

"Damn, you got it smelling good as hell in here," Cole announced as he entered the home several hours later. He smiled when he looked over at Nikki and saw her standing there naked.

"Oh, so you do know how to greet yo king when he comes home," he continued.

"It's all for you, daddy," Nikki replied as she walked towards him. She kissed his lips gently before motioning him to follow her.

Nikki led Cole to the bathroom where she had ran him a bubble bath. She had candles lit all around the tub, giving a sexy vibe to the entire bathroom. Nikki had even made his favorite drink, which she had resting on the sink. Cole smiled, not ever having anything like this be done for him.

"This is real nice, Nik. Thank you."

"You deserve it daddy, I wouldn't be where I am if it wasn't for you," Nikki spoke. She knew she was laying it on thick; however, she didn't want Cole to suspect anything until it was too late.

Cole undressed, and Nikki stayed in the bathroom while he soaked. Once he was done, Nikki rubbed his body with lotion, and Cole slipped into his silk pajamas. He felt like a king with the treatment Nikki was dishing out to him. With him being a narcissist, he was always at his happiest when his ego was being stroked, so tonight had him on cloud nine. It was something he needed, and he was overjoyed that he'd finally beaten Nikki into submission.

Nikki poured Cole another drink before they made their way into the kitchen to enjoy the meal Nikki had prepared. Nikki placed Cole's food in front of him before pouring the butter sauce on top of his lobster.

"Get me a bowl, I need some extra sauce on the side," Cole ordered.

Nikki smiled and reached into the cabinet, knowing that the more sauce he ate, the faster the fentanyl would work. Cole didn't even wait for Nikki to sit down before he started eating, stuffing his mouth as though he hadn't eaten in days.

"This shit good as fuck babe," Cole mumbled.

Once Nikki saw Cole dip the last bite of his lobster tail inside the butter sauce and then start dipping his steak in it, she knew it would only be a matter of time before Cole took his last breath. Her heart beat rapidly in anticipation as she watched Cole closely.

"Why ain't you eating?" Cole asked as he drowned a piece of steak in the deadly sauce.

"I'm just watching you," Nikki replied.

"Why? Ain't you ummm," Cole cleared his throat before trying to continue, "ain't you..." Cole dropped his fork as sweat poured from his forehead.

"I'm not eating cuz I'm waiting on you to die," Nikki stated calmly.

"What... the ... fuck... you... say?" Cole asked, stopping to take a breath after every word. He pulled at the collar of his shirt as if it would somehow help him breathe and Nikki smiled, knowing his life was coming to an end.

"Your butter sauce was laced with the Fentanyl I found in the pocket of your jeans. You're about to OD any minute now, and I couldn't be happier," Nikki replied coldly before standing from the table. "You've treated me like shit these past few months, and I refuse to let you do the same to my child. Yo ass is about to rot in hell muthafucka!"

"You bitch!" Cole yelled with all the force he could muster, knowing how deadly the drug could be.

Anger filled him, and he wanted to kill her for what she'd done to him. He'd taken her out of that roach motel she was living in, wifed her up and put her in a three-bedroom home, all for her to put a play in motion for him to be killed. Nikki had put up with more than what Cole had done to her, so he felt like the good he did outweighed the bad. He attempted to stand and go after Nikki, but fell to the floor.

His body began to seize as the mixture of fentanyl and alcohol invaded his organs. Nikki looked on in triumph as she watched the life leave Cole's body. Foam began to bubble from his mouth and he looked up at Nikki with pleading eyes. The same girl whose life he wanted to ruin just hours earlier was the one he was looking for to save his life. Nikki walked over to him, squatting down next to him and putting her lips to his ear.

"You should have just played it cool and let this just be pussy for money like it was supposed to be. But you forced my hand tryin' to force yourself into my life. Now, you don't have one of your own. I put up with enough out of muthafuckas in my life. I had to make an example out of you. See you in hell, bitch."

Cole took his last breath, and Nikki took her first breath of freedom. After months of being beaten and belittled, it was finally over. Nikki walked to the bedroom and slipped on some clothes before packing the rest of her belongings inside a duffle bag. Heading to the closet, she opened Cole's safe and fingered through the bills he had stashed there. Her heart dropped when she only counted out three thousand dollars. *Where the fuck is all the money? I know this nigga got way more than just this.* Nikki began pulling things from the closet, going through pants pockets and shoe boxes and still found nothing.

Getting frustrated, Nikki left the room and stood in the hallway. *Think Nikki, if you were Cole and wanted to hide money, where would you put it?* Nikki knew it was more money around the house somewhere, she just had to get to it. After about thirty minutes of looking through drawers and cereal boxes, a light bulb finally went off in her head.

A few weeks ago, she'd walked in on Cole hiding something in the ceiling panel in the bathroom. Running to the bathroom, Nikki stood on the tub as she reached up to the ceiling. After trying to push two of the panels, the third one finally lifted. Cautiously, Nikki felt around until she was sure she'd taken everything out of the panel. When she was done, she had found thirty thousand dollars and a bag half full of fentanyl pills. She had no idea how to sell the pills; however, she knew they were worth money, so she was going to keep them. Nikki made sure to leave a few of the pills on the kitchen table, so Cole's death would look more like an accidental overdose. Once Nikki was sure she had everything she would need, she walked out the door and made her way to Cole's car.

———

Russell drove down the street as the cool air hit his face. It had been blazing in the city that day, however, now that the sun was going down, it was starting to cool off outside. He nodded his head along to the music as he made his way home. It had been a great day for Russell, as he headed home with a pocket full of money. The girls had outdone themselves, and he planned on doing something nice for them to show his appreciation for the life-changing funds they were bringing in. Agreeing to do business with them had quickly proven to be one of the best decisions Russell had made in a very long time. Russell was so caught up in his thoughts that he almost ran the red light and caused an accident.

"Shit, I gotta pay attention. I can't be having no accidents, especially in front of the damn police station," Russell said, looking around to make sure no police saw what had just happened. His mouth dropped open as he watched Travis walk into the police station for the second time.

"This muthafucka is snitchin'. Ain't no other reason he would be at the police station this many fucking times. If I caught him twice, how many times has he been there without me kowin'. He probably the reason the police on me, now."

Beep! Beep! Beep!

The horn of the car behind him alerted Russell that the light was green, and he pressed the gas. Just like that, his mood changed as anger set in. Here he was thinking him and Travis was turning over a new leaf when really, his brother had been plotting against him. Hitting his wheel in frustration, Russell pulled over, trying to calm down. Pulling his phone from his pocket, Russell went through his contacts and tapped on Travis' number.

"What up, doe bro?" Travis answered.

"Where you at?" Russell asked.

"Shit, I'm around, just picked up my girl. You good?"

"Nah, not really. Can you come to the house tonight? I'm fucked up bad bro," Russell replied.

"Yeah, say less. I'll hit you when I'm on my way."

Russell didn't say a word as he ended the call. His emotions were running wild with both hurt and anger. Just when he thought he'd gotten his brother back, he'd shown his true colors. Russell knew he couldn't let this slide. There would be no way he was doing any time in jail, and he was gonna do everything in his power to make sure of it. Russell could only imagine the amount of evidence the feds had on him, and he knew it was all because of his brother. His blood, the one person that was supposed to have his back through it all had now became an official state's witness. Russell knew it was only one way to handle him, and that was with blood shed. Brother or no brother, Travis was about to pay the cost for crossing Russell.

Russell walked into his home with a scowl on his face that would have made anyone run the other way. *Why the fuck couldn't you just keep yo mouth closed, Travis?* Russell thought, shaking his head at his brother's betrayal.

Picking up the blunt from the ashtray on the table, Russell lit it and took a deep pull. He hated what he was about to do and it saddened him a great deal; however, he knew it had to be done. No one that spoke to the police about him were exempt and would all suffer the same fate. That was something Russell had to stand on, so he sat there, smoking his blunt while waiting from Travis to pull up.

———

Nakia laid in bed with her laptop across her lap and Raphael next to her. They cuddled up next to each other as they searched Zillow looking for homes in Mexico. Raphael sat with Nakia as they went through virtual tour after virtual tour, looking for the perfect house. All Raphael wanted to do was make sure Nakia was happy. So, if going to Mexico would do it, he was going to make sure it happened. Finally, after several houses, Nakia found two that she loved. It didn't matter to Raphael either way. He was happy as long as Nakia was happy.

"I'll tell you what, babe. Why don't you set up some appointments for us to see the houses in person this weekend? I'm sure once you step inside, you will know which one you want," Raphael suggested.

Nakia's eyes widened as a hug smile spread across her face. "That would be wonderful, but what would we do with Aden for the weekend? We can't take him to Mexico."

"I'm sure my mother or Rosa would love to look after him for the weekend. I'll call them tomorrow and make sure."

Nakia agreed and closed her laptop. She was elated by the news that she would be in Mexico sooner than she thought. *Fuck you, Agent Scott, and fuck being a state's witness,* she thought as she curled up under the covers next to Raphael and fell asleep.

CHAPTER THIRTEEN

Manny let the hot water run down his body as he showered in the small bathroom of the motel room he'd rented. Tonight was the night he would finally get his lick back and avenge the death of his only brother. After weeks of strategic planning, he was finally ready to execute. A lot of blood was going to be shed throughout the city and it would all be at the hands of Manny. He knew Niko was looking down on him smiling at the way he was about to send his killers to him. Manny and Niko would be like tag team partners. Manny would do his thing down here on earth, then send them to Niko to handle in the afterlife. Manny was ready, and after gathering his guns from the around the room, he made his way to his car. His trigger finger itched, which was a clear representation that murder was in the air. Knowing exactly how things were about to go down, Manny started his car and headed to his first destination.

When Manny pulled into Fatbar's neighborhood, he parked his car on the next street over, making sure not to be seen. He got out and armed himself with everything he would need to complete his first task. Manny showed no remorse for the crime he was about to commit. Them being family to him had went out the window the moment he found his brother dead at their hands. Knowing there were about five goons outside and not knowing who was inside the home, he knew he had to be extremely careful. Walking swiftly with his knife at his side, the black clothes he wore blended in with the darkness of the night sky.

Manny spotted one of the men walking by himself seemingly doing his rounds around the house. Manny quietly walked behind the man, not making a sound. The guard didn't even know Manny was there until it was too late. Clutching his knife in his hand, Manny plunged it into the man's neck, sending him to the ground instantly. He choked on his own blood as Manny disappeared into the night.

"Donte', are you there? Donte', come in?" Manny heard another goon speak into a radio.

Before Donte' could even answer him, Manny was on the man, slicing him clean across the throat, leaving no life in him. *Two down, three to go,* Manny thought as he went on to find another one of Fatbar's goons. Manny had not even been there ten minutes and he'd taken down two goons, and nobody had even noticed he was there yet. Walking back behind a bush, he heard the man known as Donte' answer his radio.

"You next Donte'," Manny whispered to himself. It amused him how he was coming in taking lives like a thief in the night. The men never saw him coming, and by the time they did, it was too late.

Manny watched from the bushes as two of the goons walked side by side through the grass. He pulled his gun from his waistline and attached the silencer quickly, never taking his eyes off his targets. With a marksman's precision, Manny aimed his weapon through the bushes and let off two shots, hitting both men in the head. With only one goon left standing, Manny was no longer outnumbered.

Standing from the bushes, he walked freely with his gun at his side. He didn't see the last goon but knew he was around somewhere. He contemplated just going into the house and trying his luck with the people inside. However, he'd known he'd done too much planning to just let luck take over this far in.

Once he found the last goon, it was night night for him as well, as Manny upped his Mag and sent two shots flying into his temple, sending him right over to Niko. With all the guards being dead, Manny made his way into the house through an open window in what looked to be a study. The house was quiet and he figured the family was asleep. Creeping to the door slowly, Manny opened it, allowing his gun to lead the way. His heart pounded with every step as he inched closer to his victims, excited to finally be giving them what they deserved. It was dark in the home besides the kitchen light and one of the downstairs bathrooms, so Manny headed straight upstairs knowing Fatbar and Harlin must have been asleep.

Not knowing which room the master was, Manny quietly searched every room upstairs, coming up empty-handed. Walking to the door of the last bedroom, which Manny knew had to be the master suite, he slowly opened the door and crept into the dark room. He couldn't see a thing, and a cold chill ran up his spine. Feeling uneasy, Manny rubbed his hand over the wall, looking for a light switch. Manny flicked it on, just to see the room empty.

He walked over to the bed where an iPad sat on the right corner. Manny picked it up and saw a view of the entire outside of the estate. *Damn, that muthafucka saw me coming. I should have known a house this big would have cameras. His ass gotta be in this house somewhere, though. He can run all he wants, but his ass can't hide from these bullets.* Manny thought, as he turned around and looked right into the barrel if Fatbar's gun.

"Did you think you could just come in my home, kill my soldiers and then take out me and my wife? Your own fuckin' aunt? We are your family, Manny, and you want to kill us? You had to know I wasn't gonna make it easy!" Fatbar yelled, still pointing the gun at Manny.

"Family? Nigga, fuck family! Was we family when y'all killed Niko? Or was we family when you sent me to clean up his body? You standing here talking 'bout family when y'all the ones that started this shit. Y'all took my family from me, so now you have to pay," Manny stated through clenched teeth.

Fatbar shook his head. He'd already told Manny he had nothing to do with Niko's murder. Didn't even know it was Niko's body he was sending Manny to clean up. If he would have known that information, he would have never sent Manny, and none of this would be happening. Fatbar knew it was do or die; however, he was still sad it had to come to this. No matter the circumstances, they were indeed family. Fatbar was his uncle and used to spend a lot of time with both Manny and Niko growing up.

A frown spread across his face as he remembered taking the boys fishing every other Saturday. As much as it pained him, he knew it had to be done. Without any other words, he raised his gun and sent it crashing across Manny's face, sending him to the ground and knocking him out cold.

Manny woke up tied to a chair in the basement of Fatbar's home. He could have kicked himself for allowing Fatbar to catch him off guard. Manny knew if he didn't get himself out of this, he would be in a grave right next to Niko, and he couldn't have that. With Niko being already gone, there would be no one to avenge his death. Knowing that if he died, both him and his brother's death would be in vain. Manny was gonna do everything he could to assure that didn't happen. He tried moving his hands, however, the knots were tied so tightly that he could hardly move them.

"Come on Manny, think. You gotta get out of this. These people killed Niko. They're not the same family you grew up with. They're killers and you can't let them take you out too," Manny spoke, giving himself a much needed pep talk.

After about fifteen minutes of trying to untie himself, Manny remembered the knife he had in his back pocket. *Now, how the fuck am I gonna get to it?* Manny thought to himself. Manny tried stretching his hand to reach the knife several times but couldn't grab it. Becoming frustrated, Manny let out a loud yell, feeling defeated. The basement door opened and he heard footsteps coming down the steps.

"Screaming won't get you out of here. In fact, nothing will. You won't be leaving this house alive. You see, I didn't want this, however, you've forced my hand and I have no choice but to kill you. Because of you, I have to pay for the funerals of five men and explain to their families how they were killed on my watch. Niko was an accident, and no matter how many times I tried to tell you, you wouldn't let it ride and now we're here. I loved y'all both like you were my very own kids. Do you think I would kill Niko? I would have killed for Niko and you too, and I hate the fact that you made me do this," Fatbar spoke before pulling a gun from his waistline.

Manny wasn't moved by anything Fatbar had just said as he looked at him and sent spit flying through the air, landing at Fatbar's feet. Anger shot up his spine as the disrespect had become too much. With all his strength, Fatbar punched Manny repeatedly in the face, causing both him and the chair to hit the ground with a loud thud.

"You think this shit is a game, muthafucka? You will not disrespect me like that. I have given too much to the streets to let any mutha-fucka think he can come and disrespect me. You fucked up Manny, and it's sad because your life ends here," Fatbar spoke before he walked away, heading up the stairs and leaving Manny where he laid, bloody.

He didn't want his wife to see what he was about to do to her only remaining nephew. Fatbar knew Harlin wasn't stupid, so the fact Manny had come to their home to kill them let her know what Fatbar was going to do to him. However, he didn't want her anywhere around when he did.

"Harlin, pack up a few things and go get Rosa. I don't know if he has anyone else working with him or not, but I'm not taking any chances. If he is working with someone, we're like sitting ducks in this house. You get Rosa and y'all get the hell out of here. I'm calling Raphael now," Fatbar ordered, thinking of another reason why she should leave the house.

"But, what about you? How the hell do you expect me to just leave you here?" Harlin asked, clearly shaken up. She'd heard the commotion coming from the basement. On top of that, their entire security staff had been taken out in a matter of minutes leaving Fatbar and Harlin to fend for themselves. Although she'd known Fatbar to be able to hold his own in his younger days, with him now being in his late fifties, she was afraid the stamina of her young nephew may be too much for him.

"I'll be fine. You just worry about getting to Rosa," Fatbar replied, walking out the room to call Raphael.

Harlin rushed through the home and up to her room to grab her cell phone and call Rosa. After the second call and still no answer, Harlin became worried. *Please God, don't let anything happen to my chil-dren,* Harlin prayed silently. She didn't give a damn about packing anything; her only thought was getting to her daughter and making sure she was safe.

Heading straight to her nightstand, she grabbed the .38 she kept there, along with a box of bullets. She went to the closet where they kept their safe. Opening the safe, she grabbed her passport and a few stacks of money and placed everything in her purse before making her way back downstairs.

Harlin had just made it to the top of the stairs when she heard several gunshots halting her where she stood. She waited at the top of the stairs for several seconds, hoping she would hear Fatbar's voice calling out to her. She bit her bottom lip as those seconds felt like hours. When she didn't hear anything, Harlin took her gun off safety and pointed it in front of her before she took her next step. Her heart raced and her hands became clammy. She didn't know what or who she would find downstairs, and that frightened her. She slowly tiptoed down the stairs, being careful not to make any noise. With her finger on the trigger ready to pull it if need be, Harlin stepped down the last stair and nothing was in sight. Turning to the left, Harlin walked down the long hallway and saw the bloodiest scene she'd ever saw.

CHAPTER FOURTEEN

Nikki drove down I-94 and began to merge onto 75. She didn't know where she was going; however, she knew she needed to get as far away from Michigan as possible. It was time for her to take her life back. She'd been dealt a shitty hand in life, but she would be damned if her child suffered the same fate. Nikki had never known what a mother's love felt like; however, her child would never have to know that pain. She'd never even felt her child kick, but a mother's love had already taken over to the point where she had killed to assure her child was safe and would do it again ten times over.

Nikki rolled down the windows and took in the cool breeze. It was her first taste of freedom since she'd touched down in Michigan. She smiled as she thought about how the thirty thousand and the pills she'd taken from Cole would put her up nice for a while. Once she figured out her destination, Nikki would be able to find a home for her and her child, and she couldn't wait to start her new life. With her eighteenth birthday not too far away, she knew she would have nothing to worry about.

Noticing the fuel light come on, Nikki knew she would have to get off at the next exit and get some gas. She also needed to use the bathroom, so the stop was more than needed. After pulling into the gas station, Nikki grabbed her purse that housed the money and pills she'd taken and walked inside. Her bladder was full and she rushed to the bathroom as quickly as she could in an effort to relieve herself. Nikki was still in Michigan, seeing how she hadn't been driving long, and didn't want to rest until she at least made it out the state.

Walking out the stall and going over to wash her hands, she noticed a purse on the sink. Opening it, she grabbed the wallet and went through it. The driver's license inside was of a twenty-three-year-old woman who kinda favored Nikki. Her name was Jania Savage, and there was also a social security card a debit, and cash inside as well. Nikki smiled, knowing she would be able to use the license to get herself a room when she became tired. *God must really be on my side,* Nikki thought to herself.

After grabbing a few snacks and filling up the tank, she was back on the road. After five and a half hours on the road, Nikki was finally in Louisville, Kentucky. She'd thought about stopping in Ohio but felt as though it wasn't far enough away from Michigan for her to feel comfortable. She stopped at the first hotel she saw that didn't look like it had bed bugs or roaches.

"Hello, how can I help you?" the tall blonde-haired man asked.

"Hi, I would like to get a room for the night. Just a single king will be fine," Nikki responded.

"No problem, let me get you started. For that, I would just need your ID."

Nikki went through her purse and fished out the wallet she'd found and removed the license, handing it to the clerk. He copied the information into his computer before handing the license back to her.

"Okay, your total after tax is going to be a hundred and twenty-five dollars and seventy-two cents. How will you be paying tonight?" the clerk asked, smiling at Nikki.

"Cash," she replied, taking a hundred and fifty dollars from her purse, and telling the clerk to keep the change.

Thanking Nikki, he handed her the keys to her room, and she walked away. After taking a hot shower and getting into the bed, Nikki thought about her final destination. With the ID and social security card she'd found, she would be able to get a place as soon as she knew the state she wanted to live in. She smiled at the fact she was truly getting a fresh start. *Damn, I gotta find someone to get these pills off for me, that's gonna give me even more money,* Nikki thought to herself. Nikki went to sleep that night dreaming about her new life and the wonderful memories she would make with her baby.

The next morning, she woke up feeling well rested. After years of being on edge, this was the first night she'd actually received peaceful sleep. After getting out the shower and getting dressed for the day, it was time for Nikki to get back on the road. She'd decided to drive to Miami and start a life there. Before getting on the road, she decided to fill up again and get a few snacks. She knew that she wouldn't stop again until she wanted to rest for the night, so Nikki wanted to get everything at once.

Pulling into a Speedway gas station, she parked at a pump. Nikki had her eye on every snack in the store as she rubbed her pregnant stomach. Once she was done, her arms were full with a variety of both sweet and savory snacks, along with a couple juices and bottled waters.

"Hello," Nikki greeted as she walked to the counter to checkout.

After grabbing her bags, Nikki began making her way out the store but was halted in her tracks. There standing at Cole's car were two uniformed officers. The police car they arrived in was flashing their red and blue lights, so Nikki knew then nothing good could come out of this. A chill crept up her spine as she watched them looking through the windows of the car. *How the fuck do they know about Cole all the way in Kentucky? Do they know about me, too? Fuck, Nikki, what the fuck are you going to do now?* she asked herself.

Nikki looked on in fear as she watched the officers call for back-up on their radios. She knew then that someone had already found Cole's body, probably even gave her name as a suspect. Thankfully, Nikki kept the money and pills in her purse, which she kept with her. However, all her personal items were inside the car. Turning back around and grabbing a Kentucky Wildcats cap and a pair of sunglasses, she purchased them. After putting them on, Nikki walked out the gas station and down a side street like she hadn't just pulled up in the car.

Just like that, Nikki was left with no transportation or means to get to Miami and start the new life she was just so happy about just minutes earlier. Nikki almost felt defeated until she remembered the ID and social security card that she had in her purse. *All I gotta do is find a used car dealer and get me something cheap that will get me to Miami,* she thought. Pulling out her phone, she searched the closest used car lot, which was about a twenty-minute drive. After downloading the Uber app, she took one of the credit cards from the wallet and put in the numbers.

Nikki's face lit up when the card worked, happy the woman hadn't turned her cards off yet. After putting in the address to the car lot, she waited the five minutes until her Uber arrived. Leaving her bag of food on the curb, Nikki got into the car. Once she made it to the car dealer, she walked right inside, ready to make a purchase.

"Hello ma'am, my name is Chad, how can I help you today?" the salesman asked.

"Hello Chad, my name is Jania and I'm looking for a car. I need it to be reliable but also at a good cost. I will be making a purchase today and I would love to give you this commission," she spoke.

Chad smiled and rubbed his hands together. He was one sale away from receiving his promotion. If this woman actually bought a car today, he would be going home a happy man. Chad motioned Nikki to follow him as he led her to the lot where all the cars were parked.

"What is the price range that you have?" Chad asked.

"I would like to stay under eight," she replied.

Chad nodded his head and walked her over to a 2013 dark blue Honda Accord. Nikki looked over it and saw the sticker price was fifty-seven hundred. Running her hand along the hood, she walked towards the door and opened it. Nikki sat inside and put both hands on the wheel, trying to get a feel for the car. She had to admit she could definitely see herself driving down 75 in it; however, she wanted to see the other cars he had to offer.

Next up was a black 2011 Dodge Charger. It was clean and already had tinted windows. The price on that one was seventy-two hundred, and Nikki was feeling it before she even sat inside. When she opened the doors and saw it was black on black, she was sold. She sat in the leather seat and put her hands on the wheel. Nikki knew this was the car she was going to buy and didn't need to see any others.

"I like this, I'll take it," Nikki stated.

"Great, if you follow me, we can get you set up with the paperwork for our loan program. It only takes about fifteen minutes and you will know your approval status within five minutes," Chad spoke.

"There will be no loan program, I have cash. I will give you sixty-eight hundred in cash right now," Nikki replied.

Chad thought about it for a moment; it was only four hundred under the asking price. Only a small difference in his commission and wouldn't break his pockets. With his eyes on the prize, he agreed to sell the car to her at the price she offered, knowing the sale would give him the promotion he'd been aiming for, for months. He would definitely be celebrating with his wife tonight.

"Okay, we have a deal. Let me draw up the paperwork and we can get you off the lot in no time," Chad replied.

Smiling, Nikki followed Chad into the building, taking a seat in the chair across from his desk. After signing all the necessary papers, Nikki was back on the road in her new car. It felt completely liberating purchasing her first car, and she couldn't have been happier. Losing Cole's car was only a minor setback and probably something that needed to happen. If she'd been caught driving a dead man's car, she would undoubtedly be in jail. If they knew about Cole in Kentucky then she wasn't far enough away.

Completely changing her, destination Nikki got off the freeway and changed courses, putting her new destination into her GPS as California. She stopped at a McDonald's to use the bathroom and get something to eat, seeing how she didn't want to stop anymore until she at least made it out of Kentucky. The fear of what the police might know about her was making her move completely different, and she knew she had to look different as well.

After eight hours of driving, Nikki was now in Springfield, Missouri. Not only did she need gas, she was also hungry, tired and had to use the bathroom. Once her tank was full and her bladder was empty, she drove to a nearby Burger King. While sitting in the parking lot eating her dinner, Nikki spotted a CVS across the street. She knew she would be able to find enough of what she needed to change as much of her appearance as she could. There was no way she was about to go down for murder, and Nikki would do everything she could to live the wonderful life she'd dreamed of for her and her baby.

Once leaving the CVS, Nikki found a Days Inn and pulled into the parking lot, getting a room with her stolen ID. She wanted to make herself look as much like Jania Savage as possible. Nikki didn't know who the woman was, but she was saving her life for the time being. Turning on the TV before heading to the bathroom, Nikki listened to the news as she replicated Jania Savage, bleaching her hair in order to make sure the red dye held up in her dark brown hair. Jania's hair was longer than her own. So, she figured she could just get some tracks from a beauty supply store in the morning and install them before she checked out of the hotel.

After finishing her hair and still not hearing anything on the news about Cole's death or her being involved, Nikki felt relieved. *They can't be thinking about me that hard if it's not even on the news.* Nikki decided to get some sleep, opting to get an early start in the morning. She wanted to cover as much ground as she could on her long road trip to Cali and planned to drive at least another eight hours, if not more.

CHAPTER FIFTEEN

Russell began to get impatient as he waited on his brother to arrive at his home. He'd already smoked two blunts and paced the floor two dozen times. With his gun tucked tightly in his waistline, Russell went into the kitchen to pour himself a drink. The anger he felt was substantial, and it pained him that Travis let it get this far. Russell had just finished his drink when his doorbell chimed, alerting him of Travis' arrival. A devilish grin plastered on Russell's face as he walked to the door. Russell was surprised when he opened the door and saw Arion standing next to his brother.

It's a damn shame he brought her with him; now, she gonna have to die too. Russell didn't want to kill Arion, she'd done nothing to him in his eyes, but he couldn't just leave her as a witness, so she had to go too. Russell hated the fact she'd even walked through the door, but it was what it was. Now being outnumbered, he knew he would have to come with a different approach.

"What's up bro, you said you needed to talk to me? Sorry I had to bring Arion, but some shit went down and I had her with me. I was closer to you than her house, so I decided to come here first since it seemed important. She can stay in the living room while we talk in another room," Travis stated.

Russell smiled, knowing he had to take on a friendly demeanor for the time being, even if it was fake. "Nah, it's cool, I just needed some company. The more, the merrier. Y'all have a seat on the couch, I'ma go make us some drinks. It's nice to see you again Arion."

"Thank you, same here. You have a really nice place," Arion replied, taking her seat on a couch next to Travis.

"Thank you, I'll be right back with those drinks," Russell replied.

Once in the kitchen, Russell poured Hennessey into three glasses. Pulling a small baggie of GHB from his kitchen drawer, he poured a nice sized amount into two glasses, stirring it well so the powder would dissolve. Russell placed all three drinks on a tray, placing his drink closer to him before walking back into the living room. He hated he had to do something as drastic as drugging them, but Travis had left him no choice the moment he decided to bring Arion with him.

Walking back into the living room, Russell placed the tray of drinks onto the coffee table and picked up his drink before taking his seat. He watched as both Travis and Arion picked up their drinks and sipped from them before he took a drink from his.

"So, what's up bro, what did you need to talk to me about?" Travis asked, taking another sip of his drink.

"Shit, I just needed to talk. It's been real hard around here without Hannah, and I just wanted some company. I just can't believe she gone man; I just wish I could have saved her."

"I know bro, but you can't blame yourself. You have to keep pushin' and livin' life every day. She might be gone, but you still here lil bro. Now, I'm not sayin' don't be sad because that's okay. What I'm sayin' is don't get depressed. Once you get into that shit, it's gonna be hard to get out of," Travis announced.

"Thanks bro, I needed that," Russell replied.

Arion's phone chimed, and she reached into her purse to see who had texted her. Seeing it was Deja, she replied back, telling her she was at Russell's house with Travis. Arion took another sip of her drink and began feeling woozy. Trying to shake it off, she began typing up another text.

Girl, they got be drinking and this drink got me feeling different. I think he might...

114

Arion was able to press send on the text before she passed out.

"Arion, what the fuck!" Travis screamed, quickly standing to his feet before falling to the floor himself.

Russell smiled, seeing they both were out cold. He quickly went down to the basement and got the rope he kept down there. After tying them both up, Russell lit himself another blunt and smoked it while he waited on them to wake up.

With the loss of Hannah weighing on him, he wished Travis had made better choices and not went to the police. The fact his own blood went against him hurt to the core.

"Damn Travis, why you make me do this to you, bro?" Russell asked, shaking his head at Travis.

About thirty minutes later, Travis was beginning to wake up. He tried to stand and noticed he was tied to a chair. "What the fuck?" Travis whispered.

Not knowing how the hell he ended up tied to a chair, he called out for his brother. He didn't know where Russell was or who had come in and tied him up. He kicked himself for leaving his gun in his car. However, seeing how he must have been knocked out or something, the gun wouldn't have made much of a difference anyway. Once he looked over and seen Arion tied to a chair still knocked out cold, he really began to panic.

"Arion, baby, wake up," Travis pleaded, just as Russell walked into Travis' line of sight.

"Russell, what the fuck happened? Hurry up and come and untie me."

Russell didn't say a word as he walked towards Travis. Instead of untying him, he pulled his gun from his waistline and aimed it at Travis' head.

"Russell, what the fuck are you doing? Get that fuckin' gun out my face and come untie me. I gotta see what's wrong with Arion," Travis spoke.

"Nigga, you know what I do to snitches, but somehow, you thought because you was my brother that I was just going to let the shit ride? Nigga, I don't give a fuck about blood just like you didn't."

"Snitch? What the fuck are you talkin' about; I ain't no snitch. You

got me fucked up, nigga! Now, get that fuckin' gun out of my face!"
Travis yelled.

Without another word, Russell let off two shots, each one hitting
Travis in both knees. Travis yelled out in agony as pain shot threw him.
The loud shots mixed with Travis' screams woke Arion up.

"W-what the fuck?" she asked, confused.

———

Deja woke up from her much-needed nap and went directly to the
bathroom to shower. She'd sweated so much in her sleep that she knew
she would have to change her bedding. *Fuck the bullshit, this central air is
being turned on today. It's too damn hot for this shit.* It had pretty much been
a chill day for Deja, with her task force seemingly having everything
they needed to arrest Russell. The only thing they were waiting on was
for the judge to sign off on the warrant, and they should have that by
the following morning. After months of work, the day was almost here,
and Deja couldn't wait to see the look on Russell's face when she put
the handcuffs on him.

After showering, Deja felt refreshed as she walked into her room to
change the linens. Grabbing her phone to turn on some music to listen
to as she cleaned, she saw she had a text from Arion. She opened it and
damn near fell over when she read it. Deja called Arion's phone several
times and they all ended with her voicemail picking up. Becoming
uneasy, Deja placed a call to Remy while she slipped into a pair of jeans
and a t-shirt.

"What up, doe?" Remy answered.

"Rem, something is going down. I think Arion's cover may be
blown," Deja spoke.

"What? Why do you think that? What happened? Where are y'all?"
the questions rolled off her tongue in one long breath.

"I'm at home. But Arion is at Russell's house. She texted me over
an hour ago, and I just saw it. The text said the drink he gave her made
her feel woozy, and she hasn't texted back after that. I called her a
bunch of times and she ain't answerin'."

"Okay, shoot me the address. I'll call Sophie and we will meet you there," Remy stated before hanging up the phone.

Deja immediately sent the address through text and got right in her car. She kept two loaded pistols in her car, one in her glove box and one in the arm rest. Deja also kept a .38 in her purse, so she was always ready for whatever. She tried calling Arion's phone several more times on the way to Russell's house, but her calls were still left unanswered.

"Fuck Ari, please be alright girl," Deja pleaded as she weaved in and out of traffic, trying to get to Arion as quick as possible.

———

Russell stood over his brother as he sent down blow after blow onto his face. Russell's anger was giving him a strength even he didn't know he had. Arion screamed out for Russell to stop but to no avail. Blood poured from Travis' face, as Russell continued to beat him.

"Bitch, if you don't stop all that fuckin' screamin', you gonna be next!" Russell chastised.

"What is wrong with you? You gonna do this shit to yo own brother?"

With that, Russell stopped and looked at Arion up and down. She was a beautiful woman with titties that sat up so perfect, even Russell wanted to suck on them. Walking up on her, he grabbed her breasts with his hand firmly and squeezed it.

"Are these real?" he asked, leaving a bloody handprint on her white blouse.

"Don't touch me! Are you crazy? If you untie me now and let me go, I will have mercy on you. But if you do anything other than that, yo ass will regret it. That, I can promise you," Arion spoke.

With Russell not taking too kindly to threats, he slapped her so hard that it sent her flying backwards. "See what you made me do? I didn't even want to do that shit to yo pretty ass face. Only reason you in this shit is cuz Travis brought you here with him. I ain't got no beef with you, but you was just at the wrong place at the wrong time. So, now, the way I see it, you got one of two choices."

"And what are they?" Arion asked smugly.

"Well, since you asked, you can either bring yo sexy ass over to my side and come make all my money."

"Or?" Arion asked, clearly not in agreement with his first suggestion.

"Or you can die bitch, and those are yo only two options. Now, which one is it?" Russell asked, pulling his gun from his waistline, and aiming it directly at her head.

"I don't want to die," Arion said, trying to buy herself some time. She didn't know how long she'd been out, but she knew she texted Deja just before she passed out. She had to be on her way by now.

"Then, you know what you gotta do. Get out there and make my money," Russell replied.

Arion thought for a moment before agreeing to his proposal. She knew she would never sell herself for anyone; however, she was gonna tell him whatever he wanted to hear in order to save her life. She just prayed Deja got there before he wanted to try her out for himself.

"You ready for me to be yo daddy?" Russell asked, running his hands all over Arion's body.

"Yes, I'm ready," she replied.

"Get the fuck away from her, don't touch her," Travis managed to say, spitting up blood with every other word.

Russell looked over at his brother with his gun still pointed to Arion. He couldn't believe Travis still had something to say after the beating he'd just put on him.

"Come on Russell, it's me. I've always had yo back no matter what, and this how you gonna do me? Nigga, I had yo back when nobody else did, and now, you wanna kill me? You must done became a man now, huh? Well, I remember you was so scared to pull the trigger on a nigga that was hurtin' you that I had to do it. Now, yo nuts done dropped and you wanna pull a gun on me? Well, shoot then, nigga, cuz clearly, blood don't mean shit to you!" Travis yelled. "That nigga touched you and had you doin' all kind of nasty shit while mama just let him. I'm the one that took that nigga out for you, and you wanna shoot me? Yo pussy ass couldn't shoot that nigga, though."

"Shut the fuck up!" Russell yelled at the mention of the childhood trauma he'd suffer at the hands of his mother's boyfriend.

Anger shot through his body like bolts of lightning as he listened to his brother reveal his most kept secret. For years, he'd hated his mother for what she allowed to happen to him. So much so that he blamed all women for the pain he suffered. Raheem would come into Russell's room at least twice a week for the three years he lived with him, and no matter how much he begged him to stop, he never did. It got to the point where Russell wouldn't even fight him off anymore because fighting made it worse.

When Russell finally got up enough nerve to tell his mother what was going on, she told him he had to do everything Raheem wanted. Rochelle told him that if Raheem left her because he didn't do what he was asked, she would kill him. Russell knew then that his mother didn't give a damn about him. As long as she had Raheem around to feed her drug habit, then that was all she cared about. Never mind that fact he was constantly raping her youngest son.

Russell thought back on the night Travis had walked in on Raheem violating him for the last time. He hadn't even known Travis had walked in the room until he heard the shots and felt Raheem's lifeless body on top of him. Russell pleaded with Travis not to tell anyone else what he saw because even at his young age, he didn't want anyone to look at him different after finding out he was being violated by another man. From that day forward, it was the two of them against the world.

"Nigga, shut the fuck up; I was a fuckin' kid. Ain't shit pussy about me, now. Yeah, you might of killed Raheem's homosexual ass, I'll give you that. But you left mama alive when you should have killed her, too. She was the one that let him do that shit to me. Sold her own son for a high. What you think that shit do to a little boy? To grow up havin' a mother that didn't give a shit about him. I was the one took matters into my own hands and killed the bitch that started all this. Because of that bitch, I can never love or trust a woman. Why you think I treat these bitches the way I do?" Russell revealed.

Travis' eyes widened at the realization of what really happened to their mother. All these years, he'd been left to think she died because of an accidental drug overdose, and now, he was finding out that it was his own brother. Travis couldn't believe that he'd kept this from him all these years.

"You killed Mama?" Travis asked, hoping he was hearing Russell wrong.

"Why do you look so surprised? She wasn't no fuckin' mama to me. The only thing she taught me was that bitches wasn't good for nothin' but to get a nigga what he wanted. I wanted money, so I got some bitches to get it for me. Hell, if I hadn't of killed her, that bitch would be out here suckin' dick for me, too."

Arion looked on in disbelief as she listened to Russell and Travis spill the tea on their family drama. She had no clue Russell had been raped as a child, but it did explain why he did what he did. She was glad that they were having this conversation because it was buying her time while she waited for her team to rescue her. She prayed they hurried and got there before Russell killed Travis.

"Okay, you killed Mama, and I shot Raheem for you. I had nothin' to do with what happened to you as a kid. So, why the fuck do you have me tied up?" Travis asked.

"Cuz nigga, you a snitch and thought I wasn't gonna find out. Maybe if I didn't see you comin' out of that police station today, I wouldn't have known. But the universe put me at the right place at the right time. Yo ass is a fuckin' rat, so now you gotta die," Russell replied.

"Comin' out of the police station? Nigga, why the fuck wouldn't you just ask me what was up? You so fuckin' stupid. I'm not the one against you, nigga. I was at the police station pickin' up Arion. That's why I brought her with me to talk to you cuz she was already in the car. Fuck is wrong with yo paranoid ass?"

"You really think I'm stupid, don't you? Nigga, save that shit for somebody who listens," Russell said as he raised his gun and pointed it directly at his forehead.

Just then, the three of them heard two shots and the door being kicked open. Arion smiled, knowing her girls had made it there in time to save her. Russell, however, looked shocked when he looked up and saw the red and blue lights flashing in his window.

"Russell, drop your weapon!" Deja yelled.

The sound of her voice caught him off guard, and he turned to face her. He stood there confused, looking at the three women that had worked with him and brought him so much money stand there with guns pointed at him.

"I'm only gonna say this one more time, drop yo fuckin' weapon!"

"Damn, Deja, what the fuck baby? You the fuckin' Feds?" Russell asked, placing his gun on the floor in front of him and putting both his arms up.

All this time, he thought Travis was the snitch, but it was Deja? Russell stood there confused, wondering how he'd been so wrong. Here he was thinking she was his money-making bitch, when in reality, she was a rat ass bitch. Russell had gone against everyone who cared about him because of her. He was with her when Hannah was killed and had even played her for weeks before her murder, so he could be around Deja. He was literally about to kill his brother when, all along, Deja was the one against him.

"Sorry it had to happen like this, Russell. We had a good run," Deja stated.

Russell watched, as Sophie walked over to Arion and untied her before handing her a gun from her waistline.

"Wait, so all y'all feds?" Russell asked, completely perplexed.

"We are an all-female task force formed to take lil bitches like you down," Arion replied.

'Wait, so everything we had was fake between us?" Travis asked, seemingly hurt.

"Every single second," Arion replied. "But don't worry, I'm sure the two of you will find someone in prison. Seeing how that's gonna be y'all home for a long time," she continued.

CHAPTER SIXTEEN

Rosa moaned, as Jalyn kissed her lower set of lips passionately. She couldn't believe how good he was making her feel, and she was loving every minute of it. It had been over a year since Rosa had given her body away to a man, but the way Jalyn took his time pleasing her body let her know he was deserving. Her phone rang and she pushed Jalyn's head deeper into her wetness. At that moment, Rosa didn't care about anything other than her climax.

Sitting up from between Rosa's legs, Jalyn flipped her over and slapped her ass. He watched it jiggle for a moment, then pulled her down towards him. Rosa moaned loudly when he entered her. His girth filled her like a four-course meal.

"Damn daddy, do it just like that," Rose panted.

Her phone rang again, but by this time, they were both too caught in the moment to even hear it. Jalyn was making love to her like no one had before, and Rosa was in love. He was able to go on for what seemed like hours, switching positions every so often. When it was over, they were both too spent to do anything other than lay there.

Rosa woke up the next morning and took a hot shower before heading to the kitchen. *Damn, this man got me up wanting to make break-*

fast for him and shit. He bout to make me love his ass, Rosa thought. Taking out everything she needed to prepare the meal, she began to cook.

"Damn, you got it smellin' good as hell in here. Good morning, baby," Jalyn greeted, walking into the kitchen about thirty minutes later.

"Good morning to you, too. Thanks, it's just a little something that I hooked up. Let me make the plates and then we can eat," Rosa replied.

"Damn, a nigga could get used to this shit. Do yo thang."

Once breakfast was over, Rosa went back to her room. Walking over to her nightstand, she grabbed her phone and saw she had two missed calls from her mother. Returning her call, Rosa frowned when it went to voicemail. Hanging up, she called right back and the phone went to voicemail again. *Damn ma, I know you up by now,* she thought.

Going back into her call log, she saw Harlin had called her once at two-thirty, then again at two thirty-two. The calls in the middle of the night had Rosa a bit worried, so she called Fatbar's phone. His phone didn't go directly to voicemail as Harlin's did; however, he didn't answer either.

"You good, baby?" Jalyn asked, walking into the bedroom.

"Yeah, I think so. I just can't get in touch with my parents. My mama called twice last night, and now, she's not answering the phone. I'm about to call Raphael and see if he's heard from them."

"What up, doe sis?" Raphael answered.

"Hey, have you heard from mama and daddy? Mama called me twice at two thirty this morning, and now, she's not answering her phone."

"Nah, I haven't heard from them. If she was up calling you at two thirty, then she's probably still sleeping. With all them guards daddy got around the house, I'm sure they're fine," Raphael replied.

"Yeah, you're probably right."

"Be cool, sis. I'm sure if something was wrong, they would have called me instead of you. But if it makes you feel better, I can go over there and check on them after we take Aden to his doctor's appointment," Raphael offered.

'Nah, it's cool. I gotta go out that way anyway, so I'll just stop over there. I'm sure you're right and nothing's wrong. Mama probably didn't charge her phone before she fell asleep. I'll stop by over there and see my nephew after I leave mama and daddy's."

"Cool," Raphael replied before ending the call.

"You want me to ride with you?" Jalyn asked, already heading into the bathroom to shower. He could tell that Rosa was nervous, and although he didn't know why, he knew he didn't want her to go through anything alone. So, he would be right by her side through anything that came her way.

Rosa nodded, and they both dressed and headed out. Rosa tried to push the negative thoughts from her mind, but she couldn't help but think something was wrong. As much as she wanted to believe her mom and dad were just at home sleeping, she couldn't get pass the gut feeling she had that was telling her they weren't. Grabbing her phone and calling her mother once more, she picked up speed as it went to voicemail for the third time.

"Slow down, baby. I know you wanna get there, but we gotta make it there in one piece in order for you to do anything," Jalyn stated as he watched the numbers on the speedometer hit the triple digits.

Easing her foot off the gas a little, Rosa did eighty-five miles per hour until she got off the freeway. Her hands became clammy as she inched closer to her parents' house, not knowing what she would find there. Although her father had the house surrounded by the best goons money could buy, her gut was telling her that wasn't enough.

Her worse fears were confirmed when she pulled onto her parents' street and saw it flooded with police. Tears fell from her eyes before she even made it to the house because she already knew all the flashing lights were there for her parents. Jumping out of the car before she could even put it in park, Rosa ran up to the front gate of her parents' home.

"Excuse me, miss, but you can't go in there. This is a crime scene," a female officer announced.

"What do you mean a crime scene? This is my mama and daddy's house, where are they? What happened?" Rosa cried.

She could feel her knees becoming weak and she felt as though she would fall to the ground as she waited on the officer to answer her. It seemed like everything was happening in slow motion, as EMTs ran in with stretchers and walked out with black body bags. She didn't even know when Jalyn had walked over to her, but she could feel his arms around her. He had to be the only thing holding her up because her legs felt like spaghetti.

"Ma'am, your identification!" the officer called out.

"Huh?" Rosa asked, confused.

"You stated this was your parents' house? I'll just need some identification to confirm that," the officer repeated.

Rosa reached into her purse and pulled out her driver's license. She handed it to the officer while looking around at the many body bags being wheeled away. Rosa had counted four already and that was four too many.

"Officer, where are my parents?"

"Wait right here. I'll be right back miss," the officer said in a sympathetic tone before walking away.

"Something's not right. Why is she walking away? Look at all those body bags they bringing out. I haven't seen one live person come out the house yet," Rosa cried.

"Calm down, baby. Just let the officer tell you what's goin' on before you jump to any conclusions," Jalyn replied.

The five minutes it took for the officer to come back felt like forever. Rosa saw the look on her face before she even opened her mouth and she knew her parents were dead. Tears fell, as Rosa let out the most painful scream Jalyn had ever heard.

"Miss, if you could just follow me for a moment?" The officer asked.

Both Rosa and Jalyn followed the officer over to an ambulance where two stretchers sat alongside. Rosa's entire body shook as they inched closer. The pair of stretchers housed two body bags on them. Rosa continued to cry, knowing the officer was about to make her identify the bodies of her now deceased parents. Rosa was happy Jalyn was with her because she needed to pull from his strength to be able to stand on her own two feet. When the officer unzipped the first bag and she saw her daddy lying lifeless inside a bag, she screamed out in agony, falling over onto his body crying.

"Daddy, noooo, please daddy, don't do this to me! You can't die, you're too strong to die! Daddy, get up," Rosa pleaded.

It hurt Jalyn to see Rosa like this. He knew all too well how it felt to lose a parent, having lost his at such a young age. He hated that for Rosa and wished it was something he could do to ease her pain.

"It's confirmed, that is Fatbar Gjebrea. Who is this?" an overweight white officer with coffee-stained teeth asked smugly as he unzipped the other body bag.

Jalyn scoffed at his blatant disrespect and disregard for the loss Rosa had just suffered. The nerve of these pigs, not giving a fuck about anyone. To them, this was just another day at the office, but to Rosa, this was the worst day of her life.

Rosa fell to the ground when she looked over at the other body bag and saw her mother lying inside. It was too much, both her parents at the same time? Rosa couldn't take it. Jalyn even dropped a tear as he looked on at the heartbreaking sight.

"I have some questions for you," the overweight officer stated.

"She's not up for answerin' any questions. As you can see, she's just lost her mother and father at the same time. That is a lot for anyone to handle. Rosa's gonna need time to process this before she answers anyone's questions," Jalyn replied, stepping in-between Rosa and the officer.

"I don't have time for her to process anything. I have a fucking job to do. I can't do that job without someone around here cooperating. Seeing how you two are the only ones out here breathing that are not police, she would have to answer my questions, now."

"Yo man, what the fuck is your problem? Can't you see she's griev-ing? Damn, have some respect!" Jalyn yelled.

"Richards, what's wrong with you? He's right; show some fuckin' respect. Maybe you need to go back to the precinct and do some paperwork at a desk until you learn how to talk to people," a tall man in a suit said, walking up.

"My name is Detective Abraham, and I apologize for Officer Richards. He will be leaving this case immediately. Please take all the time you need and contact me when you're ready," Detective Abraham stated, holding out a card.

Jalyn took the card and placed it inside his pocket before helping Rosa to the car, placing her in the passenger seat and getting into the driver's seat. Rosa couldn't speak, just cried loudly as she looked out the window at her childhood home, which was now the murder place of her parents. The house held so many memories; however, now when she looked at it, all she saw was her mother and father lying in body bags.

Jalyn didn't know exactly where Rosa wanted to go. However, he could only imagine that she would want to tell her brother the horrible news, so he merged onto I-94 on their way to Nakia and Raphael's house. This would be a sad day for everyone involved, and all Jalyn could do was be there for his people, especially Rosa. He could tell she wasn't gonna be okay with this for a very long time; he just hoped she didn't stay in her depression for too long.

CHAPTER SEVENTEEN

Tianna and Tiny had been working nonstop for a week and a half and now had a grand total of thirty-five thousand American dollars between the two of them. There would be no fooling them about the amount of money they had now because it was all made in the USA. They had made a pact not to stop working until they'd made it to ten clients each every day, and it had worked for them. Tiny was happy she'd put her money on Tianna because she had come through just like she said she would, and now, they were up.

It was their last day at the motel before they moved into the Airbnb Tianna had found for them. It was a nice four-bedroom house with a pool and hot tub, and they were still working like they were broke. They were both on their fifth client of the day and were just getting started. They were already at almost five thousand for the day, so they knew today would be lucrative. The first client they had that day paid them six hundred each for an hour long threesome. Which was four hundred more than the eight they charged. They had been making good money ever since.

"Girl, I'm getting' hungry," Tiny stated.

"Bitch, yo ass always hungry. Keep eating like that and you not gonna be able to work at all," Tianna joked.

"Well, shit, I gotta feed my baby. I'm 'bout to go over to the diner before my next client comes; you want something?"

"Nah, I'm good right now. If I get hungry, I'll go over there later. I'm about to hop in the shower and freshen up," Tianna replied.

Tianna got up, walked into the bathroom and undressed. Before getting into the shower, she stopped and looked at herself in the mirror. Proud of the woman she saw looking back at her. She admired herself, smiling at how far she'd come. All the people around her for the past two years had tried to take her down. She'd gone from being pimped out to turning it into her own business with girls working for her. She was beaten and sold to an Albanian brothel where she was then put on drugs and hardly made any money. She'd made it out of the brothel and was now drug free. She'd even made it all the way to America and now making her own money. Tianna was proud of herself, even if no one else was.

After getting out the shower, Tianna applied her makeup and got ready for her next John. Tiny was already back and getting ready as well.

"I was thinkin', do you really want to go to that Airbnb?"

"What you mean? That shit looked nice as hell on the pictures you showed me. And it's a whole house. Shit, I'll take anything over this small ass musty smellin' room. Are you sayin 'you don't want to go to the Airbnb now?" Tiny asked.

"Nah, I'm not sayin' that at all. I wanna get out this nasty ass room too and go to a nice ass Airbnb. I just don't know if I wanna stay in New York," Tianna replied.

"Then, where do you wanna go then?"

"I wanna go back to the D, that's where I'm from, my home turf," Tianna replied.

"Ohhh, one of them moves, huh?" Tiny replied.

"Yeah, I got some unfinished business to take care of. It's time for me to go fuck some shit up."

"Hell yeah, bitch. That's what I'm talkin' about. Let's do that shit," Tiny replied.

That night after they were done working, Tianna purchased them two one-way bus tickets to Detroit, ready to seek her revenge on Russell.

CHAPTER EIGHTEEN

Nakia went through her closet picking out everything she wanted to take to Mexico with her. She over packed her and the kids' clothes on purpose because she didn't plan on coming back to the states for a while. She knew she wasn't going to testify in Russell's trial, so there would definitely be a warrant out for her arrest if she did come back. There was no way Nakia was going to spend any time in jail when they already had the real criminal. Her phone rang and she rolled her eyes when she saw it was Agent Scott.

"Why the fuck is he calling me now? We have fuckin' days before the trial. I swear this is harassment," Nakia said, picking up her phone and silencing her ringer.

"Damn, baby, you packin' like we bout to be gone for months. We haven't even seen the house in person yet. What if we get there and you don't like it?" Raphael stated.

"I just want us to have different options when we get there, that's all," Nakia lied.

Before Raphael could say another word, they heard Jalyn screaming for both him and Nakia. They looked at each other, knowing something was horribly wrong before they both ran out the room and down the stairs. Nakia knew her brother too well and she knew what the tone in his voice meant; she just didn't know who he was gonna say died. Standing by the door at the bottom of the stairs was Rosa and Jalyn.

"Rosa, what's wrong? Raphael asked, rushing over to his sister's side.

She tried to speak, but the words would only come out as loud whales. He rubbed her back as he tried to calm her down. Raphael feared the worst as he waited for her to speak. Looking over at Jalyn, Raphael pleaded with him for answers.

"I'm sorry bro, but we just left y'all parents' house. Shit is all bad, I'm so sorry," Jalyn spoke.

"What's all bad, what are you sayin' to me?"

Nakia started shaking her head as tears rolled down her cheeks. She knew exactly what Jalyn meant, and it couldn't be more heart-breaking. Walking over to Raphael, Nakia wrapped her arms around him, trying to comfort him because she knew he was not going to take the news well.

"They gone, bro. Somebody broke into the house and murdered them and their security detail. I'm so sorry."

Raphael felt like he would fall over at the mention of his parents being murdered. He bit his bottom lip as he ran his hand over his face. He knew exactly who was responsible for the murders and he was about to take matters into his own hands. Manny was about to feel the same thing he and Rosa felt ten times over. Anger shot through his body as he punched the wall so hard, his fist went right through it.

"Baby, I'm so sorry," Nakia cried as she rubbed Raphael's back, tears falling from both their eyes as she cradled him. It broke her heart to see him this way, and she wished it was something she could do to ease his pain.

"It was Manny! He did this shit, now, this nigga got to pay. My mama and daddy damn near raised him and this what he do? It's over for that nigga for real!" Raphael yelled out in anger.

"Manny?" Rosa managed to ask.

"Yeah, sis, it's all his ass. He did this shit. He's the reason they had all that security around their house, yours, and mine. That nigga

Manny been comin' at us ever since..." Raphael paused, not wanting to add more drama onto an already horrible situation.

"Ever since what?" Rosa asked.

"Nothing, I'll just handle this shit myself," Raphael replied.

"Mama, what's wrong? Why is everyone crying?" Rashaud asked, walking down the stairs holding Lexi's hand.

"Nothing babies, y'all go back upstairs and watch some TV. I'll come up there in a few minutes to check on y'all. Everything will be okay. Y'all listen out for Aden for me until I come upstairs," Nakia replied. She watched her children walk back upstairs.

"Raphael, what the fuck is going on? Why do you think it's Manny?" Rosa asked.

"I'll tell you later. Right now, you need to stay here where you will be safe," Raphael said before running up the stairs two at a time.

Nakia didn't know what do to. The horrible news about her future in-laws had caught her off guard. It was as if their family didn't have anything except bad luck. She prayed things would get better for them, but it seemed as if every time she turned around, something bad was happening. There had to be a silver lining in all this, and Nakia couldn't wait to find it.

Nakia wanted to run after Raphael and hold him in her arms, because she knew this hurt all too well. However, she knew he needed his space for the moment. Her heart ached for both Raphael and Rose because even as adults they both spent time with their parents every day.

"Let's go into the living room where we can sit down. Can I get you anything, Rosa?"

"What I want, nobody can give me," she replied sadly before walking towards the living room.

"I need a drink. This shit is just too sad," Jalyn spoke before making his way to the kitchen.

Nakia followed behind him, ready to ask him all the questions she couldn't ask Rosa. She watched, as he poured himself a double shot of Hennessy and drank it down before she began.

"Jalyn, what the fuck is going on? Why were you and Rosa together? How did y'all find Fatbar and Harlin? And why the hell does

Raphael think their cousin has something to do with the murders? I'm so fuckin' confused about what's going on. I thought we had the security outside our home because of the man that broke in? I'm so confused."

Jalyn just looked at Nakia because half of the questions she was asking him, he didn't have the answers to. He didn't even know who Manny was, let alone why or if he'd killed Fatbar and Harlin.

"Me and Rosa been kickin' it for a few weeks now. I was at her house when she couldn't get in touch with her parents, so I decided to ride with her when she went over there. I'm glad I did because she was so distraught that she couldn't even drive," Jalyn replied.

"Wait, what? Is that the woman that's had your attention? I like this for y'all, I just wish I would have found out under better circumstances," Nakia replied.

"Yeah, me too. We were gonna tell y'all, but everyone had too much shit goin' on at the time. Man, sis, you should have seen the body bags they were bringin' out. Everyone at the house died. It was like somethin' out of a movie, sis. I ain't never seen no shit like that."

"Damn, did the police say they had any leads?" Nakia asked.

"Nah, they didn't tell us anything about any leads. To me, it seemed like they didn't know who did it."

"Then, why does Raphael think Manny had something to do with it?" Nakia asked.

"Shit, sis, I don't even know who this Manny person is, so I have no clue why he thinks that. He clearly knows somethin' that we don't."

"Yeah, let me go up there and check on him," Nakia said before exiting the kitchen.

Raphael was already coming down the stairs as Nakia was walking up, and she stopped him in his tracks. She could see the anguish in his face and wished she could take it all away. It wasn't until she looked down that she saw the two pistols he was holding in each hand. Nakia's eyes widened as the fear of what was about to take place set in.

"Raphael, what are you doing?" Nakia asked.

"I'm goin' to handle business. It's clear the police ain't gonna do shit; they probably happy my father is dead. I know exactly who did this. It's time for me to take matters into my own hands. If I would have done that in the first place, my parents would still be alive," Raphael countered.

"Babe, please calm down. I don't need you going out there and getting' yourself hurt. We have a family to take care of. If somethin' happens to you, then what the fuck are we gonna do?" Nakia asked.

"Nakia, get out my way. Somebody killed my mama and my pops. I'm not tryin' to hear about none of that shit, right now. I got some shit to handle and you betta believe I'ma handle my shit. That mutha-fucka wanted a war so that's exactly what he gonna get!" Raphael yelled.

"Why does he want a war, and why do you think Manny did this? This not making any sense to me. Manny loved mama and daddy, they damn near raised them," Rosa spoke, walking into the foyer.

Nakia looked up at Raphael, waiting for an answer as well. What did he know that he wasn't telling them? Were they all in danger? There were so many questions running through Nakia's mind, and all she could do was pray Raphael would answer them.

Raphael looked over at Nakia and shook his head before he answered. "Nakia killed his brother, and he thinks me and Pops set it up to happen. That's why the fuck he wants a war," Raphael stated coldly.

"Nakia did what? What the hell do you mean? Why the fuck would Nakia kill Niko. How did they even know each other?" Rosa asked, confused. She'd been kept out the loop the entire time, so she had no clue what was going on.

"I killed his brother? What are you talking about Raphael? I don't even know his brother," Nakia countered.

"Raphael, this not making any sense. Nakia killed Niko, how? And you knew about it?" Rosa continued.

"I didn't know it was Niko until after it happened. We ain't never had no beef before this. You know we grew up as siblings. In my eyes, those were my brothers. I guess Manny don't see it like that no more," Raphael said to Rosa before turning to look at Nakia. "You remember the man you killed in our bathroom upstairs? Well, that was my cousin, Niko. His brother Manny is who killed my Mama and Pops, and all because of you. Because of you, he thinks we set

Niko up to be killed, and that's why Manny killed them," Raphael scoffed.

Nakia was appalled to say the least and she turned her nose up at Raphael. How dare he stand in her face and accuse her of being the reason his parents were murdered? She would never knowingly do anything to hurt Raphael or his parents, so the fact he thought she did damn near broke her.

"I didn't murder a man in our bathroom. I defended myself in our bathroom and the man ended up dying. He came in this house to kill me. It was either me or him, so what the fuck was I supposed to do?" Nakia spoke.

"You should have kept yo fuckin' mouth shut, then none of this wouldn't have happened. But now, because of you, my fuckin' parents are dead. Now, get the fuck out my way, with yo police callin' ass!" Raphael yelled.

Tears rolled down Nakia's face as she shook her head. She couldn't believe the way her once so loving fiancé was speaking to her now. Would he had rather Nakia be dead instead of his cousin? Because that's the way it sounded to her. With nothing else to do, Nakia stepped to the side and allowed Raphael to pass. She wanted to stop him, but she'd said all she could say and it didn't work, so she had no choice but to let him leave.

"Bro, wait, this ain't right. It's not Nakia's fault, and I know you know that. Don't blame her for your parents' death; she's hurt by this too. We all know Nakia loved your parents. She would never put anyone in danger, let alone someone she loved," Jalyn spoke. "You need to chill on her. I know you're hurt and angry, but takin' it out on Nakia ain't the way, bro."

Raphael didn't say a word, just continued to make his way down the steps as he placed both pistols into his waistline. He had nothing but murder on his mind and he wouldn't stop until he killed Manny. He could hear Nakia crying as he walked away, but that was something he couldn't deal with at the moment. Although he did feel that she was the cause of all this, he knew she didn't do it on purpose. He just wished she would have never tried to get the police involved in business that didn't concern her.

"Raphael, wait, I'm going with you! Ain't no way I'ma let you take this shit on by yourself," Rosa called out.

Raphael didn't want his sister to come with him; however, he knew Rosa, and when she felt strongly about something, there was no changing her mind. Fatbar and Harlin were her parents too, so Raphael knew she was feeling the exact same hurt and anger he was.

"I'm not going by myself, I'm takin' the guards with me," Raphael answered.

"You and the kids need to go to Jalyn's house until this shit is over," Raphael continued, turning to Nakia.

"I'm still going with you. They were my parents, too. It's only right," Rose stated.

"Wait, what? Rosa, you don't even know what's going on. I think you should stay and come to my house with us. If Manny killed his own aunt and uncle, then he wouldn't think twice about doin' the same to you," Jalyn spoke, not wanting Rosa to be in any danger.

"I'm going Jay. This is something I have to do. If the shoe was on the other foot, our parents wouldn't rest until our killers and everyone close to them were six feet under. I have no choice but to do the same for them. I'ma be good, though. Raphael and I have each other's backs," Rosa replied.

Raphael had no further words. There would be no hug or kisses goodbye. He was on a mission. With nothing else, he opened the door and walked out with Rosa right behind him.

Nakia felt an eerie feeling take over her, and in that moment, she knew the murders were not over. There would be more dead bodies turning up, and something told her it would be someone else she loved. With her already losing the father of her two older children, she knew if something happened to Raphael, she would go insane. Not giving a damn if he wanted to speak with her or not, Nakia ran down the stairs and after Raphael, calling out to him, trying to get his attention.

"Raphael, please just wait a minute. I need to talk to you, please," she begged. If anything was to happen to him, she didn't want this to be the last conversation they had. She needed to feel his arms around her, his lips on her lips, and the words I love you. She needed him to tell her he would be back soon, so they could go to Mexico and start their new life. She needed them to be okay.

Raphael stopped and stood there with his back turned to her. He wanted to look at her, but he couldn't; it pained him too deeply. She was indeed the love of his life and the mother of his son. However, her actions had brought death upon his own mother and father.

"Raphael, I'm sorry. I have no clue how me going to work one day caused all this, but I'm sorry. I would never hurt you, you gotta believe me when I say that. I love you, Raphael, and I just want us. I want our family. But baby, we can't have that if anything happens to you. Please, don't go Raphael," she pleaded.

"I love you too, Nakia, and I'ma be cool, but I gotta go," Raphael replied before getting in the car and pulling off, with his guards following closely behind.

Nakia felt like her heart was being ripped from her chest because she knew with Raphael leaving, it meant he wasn't coming back. Not to her at least, and if he did, things would never be the same. In his eyes, she was to blame, and Nakia knew that was something he wouldn't be able to get past.

I gotta stop him, I can't let him go, Nakia thought to herself. Without another word, Nakia turned on her heels and began running towards the car, screaming Raphael's name.

"Nakia, what you doing?" Jalyn yelled out as he began running towards his sister. He knew she was hurting, but he hated seeing her like this. He'd never seen her chase after no nigga, and he was not just about to stand there and watch it now.

Nakia ran as fast as she could towards Raphael's car as she waved her hands in the air, but the car was faster than her legs. Stopping in the middle of the street, Nakia broke down crying, falling to her knees in the middle of the road.

"Nakia, sis, come on, get up. The kids done probably heard y'all and everything. Come, sis, you don't want them to see you like this. Get yoself together and let's go back and get the kids so we can get to my house. Raphael loves you, y'all got a whole family. He will be back Nakia."

"Something's gonna happen Jay, I can feel it. It was death all around that room when we were talkin'. I've lost enough people that I loved to know what it feels like," Nakia cried.

"Raphael gonna be okay sis. I'm sure he can handle himself. I'm more worried about you and my niece and nephews. We don't know who this nigga is they lookin' for. And he is clearly dangerous. We just need to pack y'all some clothes and hurry up and get to my house," Jalyn spoke.

Nakia thought for a moment. If the man she killed was Manny's brother, that meant Manny knew where she lived as well. *Wait a minute? Raphael said the man I killed was Manny's brother, so that means that man was Raphael's cousin too. Niko was sent to kill me because I called the police on that Russell guy. Is Raphael in on this shit? Was he a part of this too? Has our entire relationship been a lie?*

Before Nakia could even move, she was forced out of her thoughts by the many gunshots that began ringing out. She was so shocked that she couldn't even move. If Jalyn wouldn't have jumped on top of her causing her to fall to the ground, she would have still been standing there. She heard the car as it pulled off, but she didn't try to get up until she could no longer hear the shots. She heard another car pull up, but Jalyn was on top of her, shielding her body from the bullets. A car door opened and she heard more shots.

"Raphael?" Nakia called out, hoping it was Raphael coming back and shooting at whoever had just shot at them.

"Nakia, are you hit? Have you been hurt?" the voiced called out. "This is Special Agent Scott; I need an ambulance at 1355 Clark St. immediately. I have at least one person shot and possibly another one hurt," he continued.

Nakia became frantic at the mention of someone being shot. She knew it wasn't her because she was fine physically. However, when she called out to Jalyn to get off of her so she could get up, her worst fear was confirmed.

"Jalyn, noo! Please answer me," Nakia cried as she crawled out from under her brother. When she finally stood to her feet, she saw her brother lying on the ground. His once white shirt now stained with crimson.

Nakia had no clue why Agent Scott was there, but she'd never been happier to see him. He quickly went to work trying to save Jalyn while they waited on the EMS to arrive. A pool of Jalyn's blood began to form in a puddle underneath him, and Nakia could only pray he didn't die. She was no stranger to the pain of losing a loved one, but she knew deep in her heart that if her brother died, she wouldn't be able to handle it.

"Please save him," Nakia called out weakly. She had no strength left in her body, and all she could do was cry. She could hear the ambulance in the distance, and although it seemed as though they were getting closer, they were not getting there fast enough for Nakia.

When Special Agent Scott looked up at her with the most sympathetic look Nakia had ever seen, she knew what would be coming next. Jalyn, her only brother and the first child Nakia had raised that wasn't her own, was dead. Nakia couldn't help but to feel responsible as she dropped to her knees alongside Jalyn's lifeless body. The ambulance pulled up, but it was too late. Jalyn Pitchford would be pronounced DOA when he arrived at the hospital.

To be continued....

The State's Witness 3
Coming Soon

Did you enjoy the read?
Let us know how much by leaving us a review on Amazon and Goodreads.

KEEP READING FOR A PREVIEW OF...

The Hottest Summer Ever
By Elijah R. Freeman

PROLOGUE

Reluctant

Lighting flashed, thunder boomed and heavy rain pelted the top of the stolen Toyota Corolla as I made my way home. Feeling like time was working against me, I pushed the car past the speed limit, throwing caution to the wind. I was in a lot of pain. The adrenaline rush from my mission had subsided and the wear and tear on my shoulder was catching up to me. There was no time to acknowledge pain though. More imperative issues were on my mind. Like why Keisha hadn't told us about the unexpected visit that caused her not to eradicate all traces left by the crew. We could have done damage control before things had gotten this far.

Everyone was dead now. No wonder Keisha had backed out of the streets to go legit. She was running from her past. Her karma. Yet it found her. Her, Redd, and Polo; and there was still a loose end unattended. A loose end with all the answers to my remaining questions but would create new problems. Seeing who I'd just seen moments ago reminded me just how small the world really was. It also reiterated the fact that anything was possible and to always expect the unexpected. That along with my knowledge of Zoepound and the little I remember of what Keisha disclosed about them confirmed my suspicions and broke my heart at the same time. Redd was right.

I pulled into the driveway and sat there, trying to fix myself up in an attempt to stop the pain, physical and emotional. It was 4 am. I didn't want to do it but I grabbed my strap. My life was damaged beyond repair. Chelsea was the single thread that held it together. Without her, my whole world would fall apart. What was the point in having money if there was no one to share it with? No one from the bottom to look back with from the top. I'd spend the rest of my life in question. Wondering if the people around me loved me for me, or simply for what I could do for them. That's no way for a woman to live. A lot could've been different, and staring at the gun in my hands, all the mistakes I made throughout life came rushing back...

CHAPTER ONE

Crushed Dreams

Born and raised in College Park, it's no surprise that I turned out to be a product of my environment. I was born to Richard and Nicole Love on March 28th, 1990 at Grady Memorial, one of Georgia's prominent hospitals. At the last minute before signing my birth certificate they decided on a name, Richelle Kemoni Love. Then a few days after I was pronounced healthy, my mother was discharged and they were finally able to take me home to our small apartment on Godby Road.

I was daddy's little girl. Whatever I wanted, I got. I loved my mama, but me and daddy just always had a deeper relationship. Daddy felt children were smarter than what a lot of people gave them credit for. As a result, he spoke to me as if I was a lot older than I actually was. I was always with him, even when he would stop by some of his stash houses. He never sheltered me from what was going on, and because of this, I grew up more advanced than most kids in my neighborhood. For me, there was no Santa Clause, Easter bunny or Prince Charming. It was just daddy, my knight in shining armor. He was my everything. His every movement was geared towards providing for me and mama, and to give me the life he never had. For a while he did. My daddy, my uncle Ron, and their childhood friend, Big Rod had found a plug and was on the come up. Then one night everything changed.

I was nine when my daddy was killed. He was just starting to make a name for himself in the dope trade. The competition felt the need to get rid of him. It was the summer of '99. I was awakened from my sleep by a loud commotion. Daddy always told me never to come looking if I sensed trouble in the house. I didn't. I went to hide instead, lying flat on my back in the bathtub. Moments later there were gunshots. I closed my eyes and prayed to the heavens.

It was another thirty minutes before I left the tub and tip-toed down the stairs, peeking around corners. Whoever it had been was long gone. I made my way over to the living room, tears came streaming from my eyes. I was young but I lived in the hood and was no stranger to gunshot wounds. I picked up the phone, dialed 911, and told them my daddy had been shot. I ran over to see if he was okay. I was crying profusely. I could barely see when I knelt down beside him. "Never forget everything I taught you." Those were his last words.

"I love you, daddy. Don't leave me."

He smiled... and that was that.

When mama and the police finally arrived, daddy was long gone. Responses to calls for help from Godby were always slow.

Daddy never kept work in the house, but he was a known drug dealer. The authorities wrote his death off as drug-related. They didn't care. He was just one less nigga they had to worry about. Mama and I moved into an apartment in Red Oak Projects that daddy had in case of an emergency. Big Rod would check up on us from time to time, but my uncle disappeared. No one told me where he went, and when I asked, they acted like it was a secret or something. Big Rod took me to get ice cream often after my daddy died. Every Friday I would wait anxiously in the window for him to show up in his money green El Dorado. He would get out standing tall, big and black, putting you in the mind of Bruce-Bruce. I was always happy to see him and ran out the door to greet him, jumping up and down knowing that I was about to receive something to my childish delight. Mama liked it, too. It gave her a break.

Big Rod would lift me up, spin me around and put me in the front seat. It was on one of these days while waiting in line for ice cream at a Dairy Queens in Riverdale that some tall, bald, dark skin guy wearing blue jeans, all white soulja Reebox and a Lakers Jersey approached Big Rod and asked about my uncle.

"Heard anything from ya boy Ron?"

Big Rod shook his head. "No, and you won't either. Nobody has. I'm starting to think he's dead."

"That would be best for him," the man scoffed. He started to walk off but noticed me, and paused.

I turned to look up at Big Rod, who stared back at the man expressionless. I looked back at the man, he looked up at Big Rod and shook his head.

"That's crazy," he said.

Without another word, he walked away. Five minutes later, we got our ice cream, left, and headed to Riverdale Park where Big Rod watched me play until the sun began to set.

Weeks turned into months and as the year went on, ice cream Fridays with Big Rod became less frequent, and before I knew it, he stopped showing up altogether. That's when things changed and I began to feel the weight of my reality.

———

Mama was one of the baddest bitches in the hood until she started fucking with that shit. And yes, I do mean crack. She had a bitch ass boyfriend named Darrel who was always watching me. At ten years old, I was ignorant of the lust in his eyes and he eventually violated me. I had just come home from school and mama wasn't there, so that bastard had his way with me. She must have been chasing the best high of her life because she didn't return for hours.

Darrel was sitting on the sofa watching *Leprechaun In The Hood* when he saw me. "Hey baby."

"What the fuck? I'm not your baby," I said.

I went to my room to change clothes. I could feel the vibe of someone watching me. I turned around to find it was Darrel's nasty ass. These mere events along with the fact that he used to beat my mama were the reasons I was filled with distaste and rage when it came to him. "Get away from my door!" I yelled.

He came in, closing the door behind him. "Making big demands for someone so little."

He reached for me. I tried to run but he slapped the shit out of me. The force from his strong hand sent me reeling to the floor. I was disoriented and seeing stars as he began removing the rest of my clothes. "Just take it and the pain will go away," he spoke through clenched teeth. I was scared and tears were abundantly rolling down my cheeks. "I've been wanting this for a long time," he said, pinning me down with a rough grunt.

I tried to fight back but he was stronger than me. Every time I tried to buck on him taking off my clothes he would slap me. Eventually, he got me naked and jammed his dick inside me. He broke my hymen and tore my insides apart. It hurt so bad. I cried and screamed the whole time. Blood was everywhere.

There are some things you can't see happening to you until they do. That was the day I stopped believing in God. I was only in the fifth grade and he'd done nothing but make my life hell. I figured I couldn't be sent to hell if I was already there. I didn't tell mama. She was too *dickmitized*. Plus, he was the one bringing in what little food we did have, if that counts for anything. Thursdays and Fridays were his days off and he wanted me to be there. On the days I wasn't, he would beat me. This went on for a while until I was more than fed up with his shit.

I awoke to him arguing with mama one morning. It escalated and I came to her defense. "Get off my mama!" I was trying to pull him away from her. I never saw his hand. I felt it, it sent me flying to the wall. My mouth was bleeding and my ears were ringing.

"Leave my baby alone!" my mama screamed from the floor of our small living room.

He stomped her and told her to shut up. That's when I ran out of the living room and came back with Darrel's .38 special. With hot, angry tears pouring down my face, I screamed at the top of my lungs for him to get off my mama. He turned and looked me in the eyes.

"Shoot me, bitch, if you got the heart."

I thought about all the shit he did to me, and I pulled the trigger twice.

BWA! BWA!

His eyes were a mixture of shock and disbelief as he hit the floor, bleeding to death. The gun fell from my trembling hands. Mama screamed like Tyra Banks in *Higher Learning*. I sat on the carpet and stared at Darrel's lifeless body. The nosy ass neighbors called the police and they took me away. I did ten months in the Metro RYDC.

Mama never came to see me, let alone claim me and I was eventually placed in a group home in the middle of Hillandale, another neighborhood in College Park with seven other girls. All of them were lame as hell, except one. Her name was Chelsea. I didn't know much about her because she never talked about her past. Still and yet, for some reason, I liked her in the type of way I should've liked boys. A lot of girls hated me because all the boys wanted me, but I wasn't even interested in them, to be honest. I was attracted to pretty girls. I dressed feminine but I had more nigga tendencies than the average girl should. I guess because of the way I grew up. At least that's what I came to believe.

———

Everybody had a mentor who brought them things, except me, and when they came to visit the group home, I'd be assed out every trip. For months, I used to cry myself to sleep until one day I decided something had to shake. Now in the seventh grade, niggas would try to fuck with me but I would never buy into it. I knew what niggas wanted, and it didn't turn me on. I was repulsed by the thought of a dick inside of me. Chelsea turned me on, though. We were basically joined at the hip. She turned out to be quite gorgeous. She was a redbone with a petite frame, cute face, like one of those Disney girls, with long brown hair to frame it.

Anyway, when I realized I didn't like boys, I tended to keep a lot of female company. To my surprise niggas started to hate on me, throwing salt on my name when they could. All but one, his name was Redd. He had a light brown skin tone. His dreads were to his neck and he stood about five-nine with a medium build. His grandparents were strong believers in the teachings of Marcus Garvey, and his parents were Rootical Rastafarians who believed in the holistic way of life. While they were full Jamaicans who came to the States in the '80s, Redd grew up on Gresham Road in East Atlanta. He was a Grady baby to the fullest.

His family had come to America on a banana boat, running from the Kingston authorities. Once here, they changed their last name to Hicks and started over. Arriving in the middle of the crack era, Redd's father, Jamaica Ray, learned the recipe and went to work. He put together a crew of thoroughbreds and painted the city red. At the height of his success with Jamaican novelty shops, a Caribbean Cuisine spot, and a club called Amadu's, Raphael Hicks was born. That was two years before my time.

By Redd's eleventh birthday so much attention had been drawn to Jamaica Ray. The Feds had an ongoing investigation and eventually seized everything he owned. Jamaica Ray was arrested and extradited to Jamaica where he would never see the light of day again. Redd's mother was taken into Federal custody for several murders, conspiracy, and drug trafficking charges. Guilty with no way to escape, the woman hung herself. She was found in her cell one morning during breakfast. Redd said she was believed to have been pregnant, but he wasn't sure. It was sad.

Subsequently, Redd was adopted by a money hungry couple who didn't care how long he stayed out, what he did or who he did it with. Redd lived a lawless life. He believed that, because he was from ATL, he was above the law. He didn't take shit from nobody and his reputation made a lot of people scared of him.

Redd and I started rocking with each other. We smoked so much damn weed he started calling me Kush, and the name stuck. My girlfriends would get mad because they thought I was fucking him, but that wasn't the case. We were just cool. We even had our own secret duck off, that only we knew about, down the street from Mary McLeod Bethune Elementary. We'd meet there whenever Redd had stolen something and wanted to show off, which was often.

My first lick was with him. I was pretty fucking nervous. Not because it was my first, but because it was a dope boy named Champ. He had pull all through the city. At the age of eighteen, he had more money than most niggas his age. I mean, he wasn't Big Meech or nothing but he damn sure was plugged in. Redd didn't seem to care, so I said fuck the shit too. His spot was on the eastside and I hardly went out that way.

We went in through the window of his ground level home in Meadow Lane off Glenwood Road. We found a .380, eight hundred dollars, and some weed. Redd said it was a Quarter Pound.

Although we didn't get much, Redd let me keep the .380. That was my first strap. The money and weed were split down the middle. Four hundred was the most I ever had in my pocket. Most of my money came from females I fucked with. I had a mouthpiece for a bitch because I knew what they wanted. Chelsea would get mad when she saw me with other girls. Couldn't say I blamed her, though. I was jealous at times myself. The only difference was I never showed it. I had a reputation to keep. I could have any bitch I wanted and the ones who got no talk were green with envy.

I was jumped more times than I care to remember. I stayed getting into fights and stayed thirsty to hit licks with Redd. He just seemed to know so much. I began to see him as my only way out the hood but he saw hitting licks as his only way out. Still, we were all we had.

Available Now
On all online retail book platforms!!

OTHER BOOKS BY

URBAN AINT DEAD

Tales 4rm Da Dale
By **Elijah R. Freeman**

The Hottest Summer Ever
By **Elijah R. Freeman**

Despite The Odds
By **Juhnell Morgan**

Good Girl Gone Rogue
By **Manny Black**

Hittaz 1, 2 & 3
By **Lou Garden Price, Sr.**

Charge It To The Game 1 & 2
By **Nai**

A Setup For Revenge
By **Ashley Williams**

Ridin' For You
By **Telia Teanna**

The State's Witness 1
By **Kyiris Ashley**

Stuck In The Trenches

By **Huff Tha Great**

COMING SOON FROM

URBAN AINT DEAD

The Hottest Summer Ever 2
By **Elijah R. Freeman**

THE G-CODE
By **Elijah R. Freeman**

How To Publish A Book From Prison
By **Elijah R. Freeman**

Tales 4rm Da Dale 2
By **Elijah R. Freeman**

Hittaz 4
By **Lou Garden Price, Sr.**

Good Girl Gone Rogue 2
By **Manny Black**

Despite The Odds 2
By **Juhnell Morgan**

Ridin' For You, Too
By **Telia**

Stuck In The Trenches 2
By **Huff That Great**

A Setup For Revenge 2

By **Ashley Williams**

Charge It To The Game 3
By **Nai**

A Summer To Remember With My Hitta
By **Nai**

The State's Witness 3
By **Kyiris Ashley**

BOOKS BY

URBAN AINT DEAD's C.E.O

Elijah R. Freeman

Triggadale 1, 2 & 3

Tales 4rm Da Dale

The Hottest Summer Ever

Murda Was The Case 1 & 2

Follow

Elijah R. Freeman

On Social Media

FB: Elijah R. Freeman

IG: @the_future_of_urban_fiction

Made in United States
Troutdale, OR
11/22/2023

14832728R00096